PAIGE STARLING

AN UNADJUSTEDS STORY

MARISA NOELLE

This is a work of fiction. Unless otherwise indicated, all the names, characters, businesses, places, events and incidents in this book are either the product of the author's imagination or used in a fictitious manner. Any resemblance to actual persons, living or dead, or actual events is purely coincidental.

Cover art by Marisa Noelle

FIRST EDITION

The Shadow Keepers

The Unraveling of Luna Forester

Plastic

The Mermaid Chronicles Series

Secrets of the Deep

Quest for Atlantis

Fight for Freedom

Ghost Pirates

Vendetta

Denizens of Darkness

Vortex Returns

The Mermaid Chronicles Companion Guide

Drug Use

Prejudice – LGBTQ+

Body Horror/Mutations – Genetic modifications, experiments, or body mutilations.

For the rebels, the outcasts, and the survivors—this story is yours.

CHAPTER ONE

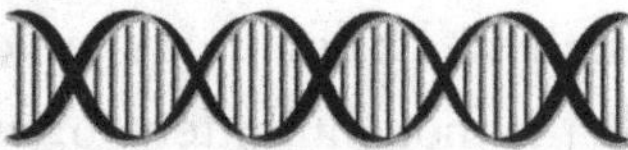

PAIGE HAS BEEN COUNTING the minutes—four hundred and seventy-three of them—since her father went through the door for the nanite treatment. Each second that passes brings him either closer to being cured or closer to...She won't let herself finish the thought. Instead, she stretches her legs across the sterile hospital waiting room and fixes her gaze on the swinging doors, willing them to open—with her father standing healthy on the other side.

"Want another cookie?" Her mother nudges the vending machine package toward her, smiling with effort that doesn't quite reach her eyes. The worry lines around her mouth have deepened over the past ten months, etching themselves into her once-flawless skin.

Paige shakes her head. The knot in her stomach has grown too tight for food. The nanite treatment—experimental, expensive, their last hope—plays on repeat in her mind. A single pill could rewrite her father's DNA, target the cancer cells, and eradicate them without the brutal side effects of the traditional treatments he's already endured. It sounds like magic, like science fiction, not something that could actually work.

Her mother's phone buzzes. "The bank confirmed the transfer went through," she whispers.

Paige nods. What's four years of university compared to a lifetime with her father? The math is simple, even for a four-teen-year-old. Still, the thought flutters through her mind that her future has suddenly become less certain, traded for her father's. She pushes it away. Selfish thoughts aren't welcome today.

The diagnosis struck ten months ago, thundering into their lives like a wrecking ball. Stage four pancreatic cancer. The words still make Paige's chest tighten, squeezing the air from her lungs as effectively as they did the first time the doctor spoke them.

She remembers her father sitting at the kitchen table that evening, his shoulders slumped in a way she'd never seen before. He'd always been larger than life—coaching her soccer team, spinning her mother around the kitchen to invis-ible music, hoisting Paige onto his shoulders even when she protested, "Too old for that, Dad." Cancer had shrunk him somehow, even before the weight loss and the treatments began.

"We'll fight it," he'd said, his voice cracking. "Every step of the way."

And they had. Chemo left him vomiting for days. Radiation burned his skin raw. Experimental immunotherapy gave him hives and fevers but did nothing to shrink the tumors. Until last week, when their oncologist had mentioned the nanites. The treatment had been around for a while, but it was expensive, and if it didn't cure you, it could kill you.

"It's not cheap," the doctor had warned.

Her father had laughed, a hollow sound. "What part of cancer is?"

Now, four hundred and seventy-eight minutes into waiting, the doors finally swing open. The doctor emerges first, and Paige's heart stops at the smile on his face. A real one, not the pitying grimace they've grown accustomed to.

"It took," he says simply.

And then her father walks through the door.

Paige's breath catches. He's standing straighter than he has in months, the yellowish tint to his skin already fading. His eyes—her eyes, emerald green and deep as forest pools—sparkle with something that looks suspiciously like hope. When he sees them, his face breaks into a grin that transforms him from the shell he'd become back into the dad she remembers.

"There's my girls," he says, arms outstretched.

Paige doesn't remember moving, but suddenly she's engulfed in his embrace, breathing in the hospital antiseptic and beneath it, the scent that is uniquely her father—cedar and coffee and home. Her mother joins the huddle, her slim arms encircling them both, and for the first time in ten months, they feel like a complete unit again.

"How do you feel?" her mother asks, voice trembling.

"Like I could run a marathon," he says, and there's wonder in his voice. "The pain...it's just gone. Like someone flipped a switch."

The drive home feels like a victory parade. Her father insists on stopping for ice cream. "Doctor's orders, gotta put on some weight."

They eat it in the car, laughing as it drips onto the leather seats her mother has always been so particular about. Paige savors the sweetness, the cold rush against her teeth, but mostly she relishes the sound of her father's laugh, unrestrained and full-bodied the way it used to be.

At home, they order in from all their favorite restaurants. Chinese and pizza and Thai, a feast to celebrate life reclaimed. Her father eats with gusto, something he hasn't done in months, and Paige feels something loosen in her chest.

"To nanites," her father toasts, raising his glass of beer. "The miracle of modern science."

They clink glasses, and Paige sips, but there's a flicker of unease beneath her joy. She's heard things about nanites at school, whispered conversations about kids who used them for enhancements rather than medical necessities. She's seen the effects too. How they've changed, become obsessed with the next upgrade, the next improvement. How friendships splintered between the "adjusteds" and "unadjusteds." How Renee now has butterfly wings, and Josh has bulked up with armored skin, and Pippa can run faster than a bullet.

But those were cosmetic nanites, she reminds herself. This was different. This was survival.

"What does it feel like?" she asks. "The nanite?"

Her father considers, chopsticks paused midair. "Like...imagine having a million tiny workers inside you, all focused on fixing what's broken. You can almost feel them buzzing around, rebuilding." He smiles. "Like magic, but science."

Later that night, after her mother falls asleep on the couch, Paige sits with her father on the back porch, watching the stars come out one by one. Crickets chirp in the grass. The sound of a dog barking in a distant yard reaches her ears. A few shouts from local teens prowling the neighborhood interrupt the peaceful night.

"I'm sorry about your college fund," he says quietly. "We'll build it back up. I promise."

Paige shrugs. "It's okay. I'm just glad you're here."

"I'm not going anywhere now, kiddo." He wraps an arm around her shoulders, pulling her close. "This is our second chance. Everything goes back to normal now."

She leans into him, finally letting go of all the stress she's been carrying for the last six months.

"Mom said they're running tests later this week to confirm the cancer is gone?"

"Just a formality. I can feel it, Paige. Whatever those nanites are doing, it's working. I'm back." He squeezes her shoulder. "And I won't waste a minute of it."

When she finally goes to bed, Paige lies awake staring at the glow-in-the-dark stars her father helped her stick to her ceiling when she was eight. The constellations they created together—some real, some invented—shine down on her like promises.

She thinks about what it means to be whole again. About the college fund that will be replenished. About family dinners and soccer games and her father growing old enough to see her graduate, marry, have children of her own. All the futures that were fading from possibility now restored by a single pill, a microscopic army rebuilding what cancer tried to destroy.

Nanites. The word rolls around in her head, fascinating and slightly terrifying. One small thing that changed everything.

CHAPTER TWO

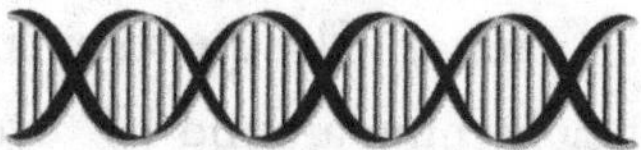

THE FIRST SIGN comes three months after the cancer nanite, so subtle Paige almost misses it. Her father lingers in front of the bathroom mirror, fingers tracing the hollows beneath his cheekbones where illness carved away at him.

"Still look a bit...depleted, don't you think?" he asks no one in particular, but his eyes find Paige's in the reflection. She shrugs, unsure what to say. He looks alive—shouldn't that be enough? But the way his gaze stays fixed on his own reflection a beat too long makes something flutter uneasily in her stomach.

She dismisses it. He's been through hell. Of course he's hyper-aware of his body now; it betrayed him once. He's just making sure it doesn't happen again.

A week later, he comes home with a small paper bag from NanoTech, the same place they got the cancer nanite. Paige lifts her head from her tablet where she's doing homework at the kitchen table to see him pull out a tiny silver packet, holding it up to the light like it's a precious gem.

"What's that?" she asks, pencil hovering over her algebra.

"Just a little pick-me-up." He grins, and she notices how his teeth have a slight yellowish tinge—a side effect of some of the cancer treatments. "Nothing major. Just thought I'd fix these chompers."

Her mother walks in from the garden, dirt still clinging to her knees. "Is that a nanite?" The question is casual, but Paige catches the slight tightening around her eyes. "Is everything okay with the cancer?"

"Perfect. Clean bill of health." He shakes the packet. "This is just...cosmetic. Those treatments did a number on my teeth. Figured while we're still paying off the medical bills, might as well look the part of a healthy man."

Her mother nods, but the worry doesn't leave her face. "How much?"

"Barely even register it," he says, waving away the question as he fills a glass of water. "Basic model. Just gets them white again, nothing fancy."

He swallows the nanite with a dramatic gulp, then smacks his lips. "Done! In twenty-four hours, I'll have a smile to rival those actors on the digiboards."

Paige watches him carefully. There's something different in his energy. A buzz, an excitement that seems disproportionate to whiter teeth. But maybe it's just relief. Maybe it's just happiness at reclaiming pieces of his pre-cancer self.

"Your teeth look fine, Dad," she says.

He winks at her. "They'll look better tomorrow."

And they do. Blindingly white, like fresh snow under direct sunlight. Her father can't stop smiling, flashing his new teeth at everyone—the mail carrier, the neighbors walking their dog, the grocery store clerk. Paige notices how often he checks his reflection now, in windows, in the toaster's chrome surface, in his phone camera.

"It's a little weird, right?" she asks her mother one afternoon while they fold laundry. Her father is out for a run. It's another new habit, part of what he calls his "rebirth regimen."

Her mother hesitates, matching socks with measured precision. "He's been through a lot. If this makes him happy..."

"But it wasn't necessary," Paige says. "Not like the cancer nanite."

"Sometimes what we need and what makes us feel better aren't the same thing." Her mother smiles, a smile that remains isolated to her lips. "Let's give him this. He deserves to feel good about himself again."

Paige nods, but the uneasiness doesn't leave her. She thinks about the kids at school who have taken enhancement nanites, how they cluster together at lunch, trading stories about their latest upgrades like they're discussing new smartphones.

Carson is the only one who gets it. But he thinks if he takes a speed or bulk nanite, people will stop suspecting he is gay. The number of times they've debated that in the tree-house they built a few summers ago is enough to make Paige's head ache with the memory of the arguments.

He should just accept who he is. And other people should too. And if they don't like it, they can lump it. He says her view is too naïve. That it's not her who is gay. That it's not her who has whispers spread about her around the school, it's not her who's excluded from the jocks' table at lunch—not that that matters as they always sit together—it's not her they make memes about and spread them through the school's chat groups.

Paige doesn't understand why everyone has to get up in everyone else's business. Why can't people just be left in peace?

These thoughts go around and around her head for a couple weeks as she watches more classmates take nanites and sprout wings, or horns, or beaks, or shells, or whatever the hell ungodly combinations they can come up with.

"No more sunscreen!" her father announces one afternoon. He shows off his golden-brown skin that looks like he's spent a month at the beach rather than working in his office. He poses in front of the mirror, turning to examine himself from different angles. "What do you think? Too much? Not enough?"

It looks artificial—too uniform, too perfect—but she shrugs. "Looks good, Dad."

Then comes the metabolism booster. "It'll help me process nutrients more efficiently," he explains over dinner, though he's barely touching the food her mother spent hours preparing. "The salesperson said it's popular with athletes. Helps them bounce back faster."

"You're not an athlete, honey," her mother points out gently.

"Not yet." He winks, and there's something unfamiliar in his expression—a smugness that doesn't fit the father she knows. "But now I've got a second chance, why not become the best version of myself?"

The best version. The phrase nags at Paige. What was

wrong with the version that read her bedtime stories and taught her to ride a bike? The version that cried at her school play and fell asleep on the couch watching old movies? That version had been dying, she reminds herself. That version needed saving.

But this new version is becoming someone else entirely.

Paige spends more time in the treehouse with Carson. Deep in the woods. No one else knows it's there. High up in the trees. They keep snacks and drinks and pillows and blankets. They could spend the whole summer there if they want to. Maybe they will. Over the years, she's built up the muscles in her arms from climbing the rope ladder. But damn, a pair of wings would make things easier.

She laughs at the thought. No way. *No freaking way.* Wings might be one of the more beautiful nanites, but they're also one of the most expensive. And there's no way she's draining the rest of her college fund.

By the time school lets out for summer break, her father has taken a fat-reduction nanite. His body, once softened by middle age and then hollowed by illness, now looks sculpted, every muscle defined as if carved from marble.

"Your dad is looking...different," her friend Lexi comments when she comes over to study. They watch through the window as her father washes his car, shirtless in the summer heat, muscles rippling with each movement. "Like, hot different."

Paige grimaces. "He's obsessed with these enhancements. Spends hours looking at himself."

"My cousin's dad is like that too. Started with hair regrowth, ended up with retractable claws and infrared vision." Lexi shrugs. "They're divorced now. Her mom couldn't deal with the changes."

The comment settles like a stone in Paige's stomach.

That Saturday, her parents throw a cookout for the neighborhood. Her father's idea. "Time to reintroduce myself to the world," he says, arranging platters of food he won't eat thanks to his new "optimized digestive system."

Paige watches from the corner of the deck as her father holds court, a group of neighbors gathered around him like moths to a flame. He's telling the story of his cancer, a narrative that's evolved from humble gratitude to something that sounds almost like a superhero origin story.

"The nanites basically rebuilt me from the inside out," he says, flexing an arm casually. "And after I beat death, I thought, why stop there? Why not see what this technology can really do?"

One of the women, the divorcée from three doors down, touches his bicep admiringly. "Well, whatever you're doing, it's working."

Paige's mother stands at the edge of the gathering, a frozen smile on her face, the plate of hamburger buns she's holding seemingly forgotten. She was a model in her youth. Has still retained much of her beauty, but hasn't worked in years. Such is the harshness of the industry and people being passed over as soon as they hit thirty. But Paige thinks her mom is beautiful, thinks she could model skin care products for older woman. But then there are nanites for that. No one buys moisturizer anymore.

Later that week, Paige is taking out the trash when she notices the recycling bin overflowing with NanoTech packaging. She counts at least five different nanite packets, some with labels she doesn't recognize. Cellular regeneration. Collagen boosting. Optical enhancement for night vision. Each more expensive than the last, based on the gold and platinum trim on the packages.

At dinner that night, the silence stretches between them, taut as a wire. Her father, absorbed in his food—a specially formulated protein mix that's supposed to optimize muscle development—barely looks up. Her mother pushes pasta around her plate, eyes fixed on a point somewhere beyond the table.

"I saw the NanoTech packages," Paige finally says. "How many nanites are you taking?"

Her father looks up, surprised, as if he'd forgotten they were there. "Just a few supplements. Nothing major."

"Five isn't a few," Paige counters. "And they don't look like supplements. They look expensive."

Her mother sets down her fork. "Silas, we talked about this. We agreed to pace ourselves with the expenses after the medical bills."

"And we will," he says, but his attention is already drifting back to his protein mix. "But these are investments, not expenses. Better health means higher productivity. Higher productivity means more money." He grins, teeth flashing unnaturally white. "Besides, you can't put a price on feeling good about yourself."

"Actually, there's literally a price tag on each nanite," Paige mutters.

Her father ignores the comment. "In fact, I've got something to show you both." He stands up, unbuttoning the top of his shirt to reveal a thin, luminescent band around his throat, pulsing with a soft blue light. "Just got it today. Heartbeat visualizer. See how it flashes with each beat? The salesperson said it's the hottest new thing in LA."

The light pulses hypnotically, casting blue shadows across his face. It makes him look alien, not like her father at all.

"We're a long way from LA, honey," her mom says.

"Why?" The question bursts from Paige before she can stop it. "Why would you need that?"

He looks genuinely puzzled by her reaction. "Why not? It's cool. Makes me feel...alive." He touches the glowing band almost reverently. "After coming so close to death, being able to see my heartbeat, to show it to the world...it's powerful."

"It's unnecessary," her mother says quietly.

"So are those earrings you wear," he shoots back, a defensiveness entering his voice that Paige hasn't heard before. "So are half the things we own. But they make us happy. This makes *me* happy." He looks between them, the blue light pulsing faster with his rising heartbeat. "Why can't you be happy for me?"

The question hangs in the air, unanswered. Because the truth is too complicated, too frightening to put into words. Because the father sitting across from them, with his perfect teeth and sculpted body and glowing neck implant, is becoming a stranger before their eyes. And neither Paige nor her mother knows how to reach the man who's disappearing behind the enhancements, one nanite at a time.

CHAPTER THREE

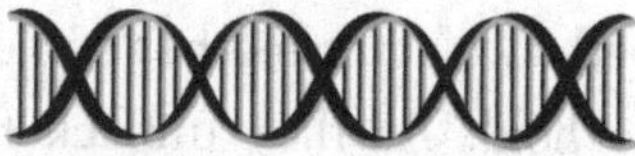

THE STATEMENT ARRIVES in the mail on a Tuesday, addressed to both her parents but somehow landing in Paige's hands as she sorts through the stack of envelopes. College Education Fund, the header reads, and below it, in stark black numbers that make her stomach drop, a balance that's less than half what it was six months ago. Paige stares at the paper, willing the numbers to change, to shift, but they remain stubbornly fixed. Fifty-five thousand dollars...gone, vanished like smoke. The cancer treatment took a chunk. That she understood, accepted, even embraced. But the rest? The withdrawals after his recovery? Those are harder to explain away.

She traces the dates with her finger. Three days after the teeth whitening nanite: $1,500. A week later, the tan: $2,200. The metabolism booster: $4,800. The fat reducer: $4,000. The neck implant: $5,750. And a dozen smaller withdrawals for nanites she doesn't even recognize.

The front door opens, and Paige quickly folds the statement, tucking it into her pocket. Her mother enters, arms laden with groceries, face tight with the strain that's become her permanent expression over the past months.

"Need help?" Paige asks, already moving to take some of the bags.

"Thanks, sweetheart." Her mother smiles, a fragile thing that doesn't quite hold. As they unpack the groceries—all organic, all specifically chosen to complement her father's nanite-enhanced digestive system—the statement burns a hole in Paige's pocket.

"Mom," she finally says, setting down a carton of eggs. "I found something in the mail today."

Her mother's hands still over a bunch of kale. "Oh?"

Paige pulls out the statement, unfolding it carefully as if it might bite. "My college fund is...there's less than half of it left."

She watches her mother's face, expecting shock, outrage, something. Instead, there's only a quiet resignation that's somehow worse.

"I know," her mother says, her shoulders sagging. "I've tried talking to your father about it, but he..." She trails off, looking out the window where they can see her father in the driveway, washing his car again. His third time this week. His muscles gleam in the sunlight—too sculpted, too perfect. "He says it's an investment in our future. That with his 'improvements,' he'll be able to earn it all back and more."

"Do you believe him?" Paige asks, though she already knows the answer.

Her mother turns back to the kale, tearing it into pieces with more force than necessary. "I want to."

The non-answer settles between them like a weight.

"It's my future," Paige says, her voice smaller than she intended. "That money was for college."

"I know, sweetheart." Her mother abandons the kale to wrap an arm around Paige's shoulders. "And we'll figure it out. I promise. Your education is still a priority. Maybe I can go back to work, or—"

"Or Dad could stop spending thousands on turning himself into something he's not," Paige cuts in, surprised by the bitterness in her voice.

Her mother doesn't contradict her, which speaks volumes.

That evening, Paige sits on her bed, rehearsing what she'll say to her father. The words tumble through her mind, rearranging themselves into different configurations, none of them quite right. How do you tell someone you love that they're becoming unrecognizable? That they're trading your future for their vanity?

She remembers the night after his first treatment, sitting on the porch and looking at the stars. "Everything goes back to normal now," he'd promised. "I'm back."

But he wasn't back. Not really. The man who returned wasn't her father—not completely. Or maybe the nanites just revealed a part of him that had always been there, dormant until tragedy and technology combined to bring it to the surface.

She takes a deep breath and stands up. No more hiding.

No more pretending things are okay when they're clearly spinning out of control.

She finds him in his study, bent over his tablet, scrolling through what looks like a catalog of body modifications. The blue pulse from his neck implant casts an eerie glow on his face, highlighting cheekbones that are now impossibly sharp, a jawline that looks like it could cut glass.

"Dad?" she starts. "Can we talk?"

He looks up, and for a moment—just a flicker—she sees recognition in his eyes, the father she remembers. Then it's gone, replaced by a distracted smile. "Sure, sweetheart. Just give me a minute. I'm researching something."

Before she can say more, the doorbell rings. Her father jumps up, suddenly animated. "That must be it!" He brushes past her without another glance.

Paige follows him to the door, where a delivery person hands over a small package bearing the now-familiar NanoTech logo.

"Finally," her father breathes, tearing into the packaging right there in the doorway. Inside is a silver case, which he opens to reveal three nanite packets nestled in velvet, each with a platinum trim that Paige knows means top-of-the-line. Expensive.

"What are those?" she asks, though she's not sure she wants to know.

"The future," he says, holding one up to the light. The pill inside glimmers with an iridescent sheen. "This one's for enhanced vision. Not just better eyesight, but the ability to see in infrared. And this," he holds up another, "will give me improved reflexes. Thirty percent faster reaction time."

The third one he doesn't identify, but his eyes linger on it with an intensity that makes Paige shiver.

"How much?" she asks.

He waves a dismissive hand. "Let me worry about that."

"I am worrying," she insists. "Because it's my college fund paying for all this, isn't it?"

But he's already walking away, the nanites clutched in his hand like precious treasure, her question hanging unanswered.

Paige hides in her room until voices flood the house. She pops her head out to find her dad in the middle of hosting a small gathering, men from work and the gym, all of them sporting various enhancements of their own. Horns protruding from temples. Fingers that extend into impossible lengths. Eyes that shift color with mood changes. Paige observes from the staircase, out of sight but close enough to hear.

"You think the reflexes are impressive, wait till you see what's next," her father is saying, the blue pulse at his neck racing with excitement. "I'm thinking about scale integration. Reptilian DNA spliced in to create armor over vital organs."

One of the men whistles. "That's high-end. NanoTech's premium line, right? Gotta be what, twenty, thirty grand?"

Her father shrugs, swirling amber liquid in a glass. "Worth every penny. In this economy, you can't afford to be purely human anymore. Not if you want to compete."

The words hit Paige like a physical blow. Purely human. As if that's a deficiency to be corrected rather than the essence of who they are.

She retreats to her room, the conversation swirling in her

head along with calculations she can't avoid. Twenty to thirty thousand for the next enhancement. There will be nothing left of her college fund.

The next morning, she waits until her mother leaves for her therapy appointment. It's another new expense, but one Paige can't begrudge given what their family is going through. Then she corners her father in the kitchen as he mixes his protein shake.

"We need to talk about my college fund," she says, determined not to be brushed off this time.

He barely glances up from the blender. "What about it?"

"More than half of it is gone." She keeps her voice steady, refusing to show how much this hurts. "And I know where it went. The nanites. All of them."

The blender whirs to life, drowning out whatever response he might have given. Paige waits, counting the seconds until he turns it off. When he finally does, she continues before he can change the subject.

"You promised we'd rebuild it after the cancer treatment. But instead, you're draining what's left." She pulls out the statement, which she's been carrying like a talisman. "See for yourself."

He glances at it, then takes a sip of his shake. "It's an investment, Paige."

"In what? Seeing in the dark? Flashing neck jewelry? How does any of that help my future?"

A flicker of irritation crosses his face. "In myself. In my potential. Do you have any idea what these enhancements can do for my career? For my earning potential?" He taps the pulse point at his neck. "This isn't vanity. It's strategy."

"It's my education money," Paige insists. "My future."

"And I'll get it back tenfold," he says, his voice taking on the smooth, rehearsed quality she's come to associate with his nanite justifications. "These enhancements make me more productive, more creative, more valuable in the marketplace. I've already lined up three new clients because they were impressed with my forward-thinking approach. That's how business works now, Paige. Adapt or get left behind."

"That doesn't sound like a sure thing," she says, trying to match his logical tone even as her heart races. "It sounds like a gamble."

He laughs, a sound that doesn't reach his enhanced eyes. "Life is a gamble, sweetheart. nine months ago, I was gambling with whether I'd even have a future. Now I'm building a better one for all of us." He drains his shake and sets the glass down with finality. "Trust me. The money will come back. And more."

"But what if it doesn't?" she presses. "What if you spend it all and—"

"It *will*." His voice hardens, the blue pulse at his neck speeding up. "You think I'm being selfish, but everything I do is for this family. To make us stronger. To protect us."

"From what?" Paige asks, genuinely confused. "The cancer's gone. We were supposed to go back to normal."

"Normal?" He laughs again, but there's no humor in it. "Normal is what almost killed me. Normal is weakness. Vulnerability." He gestures to his enhanced body. "This is the future, Paige. And I'm securing our place in it."

The conviction in his voice is absolute, brooking no argument. This isn't a discussion; it's a declaration. Her father—or the man wearing a version of his increasingly modified face—has made his decision.

"I have a meeting," he says, checking the time on a watch that probably cost as much as a semester of college. "We'll talk more about this later."

But they both know they won't. The conversation is over, her concerns dismissed as easily as swatting away a fly.

After he leaves, Paige sits at the kitchen table, staring at the college fund statement. The numbers blur as tears fill her eyes. She thinks about the father who promised to rebuild her fund, who told her everything would go back to normal. Who looked at the stars with her and spoke of second chances.

That man fades a little more with each nanite, replaced by someone she hardly recognizes. Someone who values enhancement over education, modification over memory. Someone who thinks being "purely human" is a weakness to be corrected.

The realization settles over her like a shroud: her father survived cancer only to lose himself to something equally insidious. And now her future is collateral damage in his transformation.

She folds the statement carefully and places it back in its envelope. There will be no convincing him, no breaking through the barrier of self-justification he's built around himself. She will need to find another way—another path to her future that doesn't depend on nanite-driven promises of tenfold returns.

As she heads upstairs to her room, she passes a mirror in the hallway and catches sight of her reflection. Purely human, her father called it. A deficiency. She studies herself

—her emerald eyes (his eyes, before the enhancements started changing them), her long dark hair, her unmodified skin. She is her father's daughter, but she is also herself. And she will not let his obsession define her future.

Not if she has anything to say about it.

THE DINING ROOM chandelier throws prism patterns across Paige's mashed potatoes, like the fractured relationship with her parents that started two years ago. She pushes food around her plate, avoiding eye contact with her father, whose antlers scrape against the ceiling every time he leans back in his chair. His heartbeat necklace implant pulses beneath his skin—throbbing blue, then red, then blue again—casting an eerie glow on the sterling silver cutlery her mother insists they use for every meal now, as if expensive tableware might distract from the fact that they're falling apart.

"Paige, darling, you've barely touched your dinner," her mother chirps through the beak that has replaced her mouth, a glossy, curved appendage that makes her words come out with a slight whistle. She tilts her head in that birdlike way that's become her signature move since the transformation. Her feline eyes, with vertical slits for pupils, narrow with what Paige assumes is concern, though it's hard to tell with her mother's face being more animal than human these days.

"I'm not hungry," Paige says, the same words she's repeated nearly every night for months. Truth is, she's starving, but she'd rather wait and eat alone in her room than sit through another excruciating family dinner.

Her father clears his throat, the sound deeper and more guttural than it was before the bear DNA alteration he took last summer. "You know, when I was battling cancer, I would have given anything to have an appetite." He gestures with his fork, his hand sporting elongated fingers to support a passing hobby of learning the piano. The instrument has been gathering dust for over a year now. "I fought to survive so we could have moments like this as a family."

Paige swallows the retort forming in her throat. Her father's cancer card is the ultimate conversation stopper. When he was diagnosed, she'd been terrified of losing him. When the regeneration nanite cured him, she'd been grateful, relieved. She couldn't have predicted how that pill would become the first domino in a cascade that would transform her parents into unrecognizable creatures who she shares nothing with but DNA.

"I know, Dad." The words taste bitter on her tongue. "I just have a lot of homework."

"School, school, school." Her mother's blue shoulder horns twitch with agitation, the movement rippling across the iridescent scales that now cover her upper back. "There's more to life than academics, Paige. Look at me, I was scouted at seventeen. My face was my fortune." She preens, stroking the feathery filaments that have replaced her hair. "And now, with these enhancements, I'm booking more modeling jobs than ever."

Paige nods, not bothering to point out that her mother's "jobs" now consist primarily of avant-garde photoshoots for underground magazines that fetishize extreme body modifications. The glossy framed covers line the hallway upstairs, her mother's new shrine to herself.

"Speaking of academics," her father says, leaning forward, antlers tilting dangerously close to the crystal light fixture, "I checked the college fund today."

Paige's stomach clenches. This conversation never goes well.

"And?" she asks, though she already knows the answer.

"Well, we had to make a small withdrawal." His implant pulses faster, the rhythm betraying his excitement. "New opportunity came up. A limited-edition bone-density nanite. Makes your skeleton virtually unbreakable." He thumps his chest. "Important for a man my age."

"How much is left?" Paige keeps her voice steady, gripping her fork tighter.

Her father shifts, his massive frame making the designer chair creak. "Around two thousand."

The room spins slightly. Two thousand dollars. From the fifty-five thousand that was there on her fourteenth birthday. Two thousand dollars won't cover a semester's worth of textbooks, let alone tuition.

"You promised," she whispers, the words escaping before she can stop them. "You promised that fund was untouchable."

Her mother waves a dismissive hand, the light catching on her talon-like fingernails. "Oh, Paige, don't be so dramatic.

Two thousand is plenty to start with. Your father puts money in all the time."

"And takes it right back out," Paige says.

Her father's expression darkens, the implant in his neck flashing an angry crimson. "Now listen here, young lady. I've told you before, college is becoming obsolete anyway. Why spend four years learning redundant skills when one pill can give you everything you need to succeed?"

"Because I don't want nanites." The words hang in the air between them, heavy with implication. "I don't want to change who I am."

Her mother laughs, the sound distorted through her beak. "Everyone changes, darling. It's called evolution. These," she gestures to her horns, "are just speeding up the process."

"It's not evolution if it happens overnight," Paige mutters.

Her father slams his hand on the table, making the dishes jump. "That's enough. This attitude of yours is getting tiresome. You're sixteen, Paige. Not long until you'll be an adult, and the world has no place for unenhanced people anymore." He leans across the table, his breath hot against her face. "President Bear himself has said the future belongs to the altereds."

"President Bear," Paige repeats, unable to keep the disdain from her voice. "The man who shoots venomous webs from his palms and wants to lock up anyone who refuses nanites."

"He's visionary," her father insists, his voice rising. "He understands that strength comes from adaptation."

"He's a monster," Paige says quietly.

Her mother gasps, the sound whistling through her beak. "That's treason!"

"It's an opinion," Paige counters, pushing her chair back. "Can I be excused?"

Her parents exchange a look, one of those silent communications that seems to say: Where did we go wrong with her?

"Fine," her father finally says. "But this conversation isn't over. The enrollment period for the Young Patriots Enhancement Program opens next week. Three free nanites of your choice." His eyes gleam with fervor. "Think about it, Paige. You could have wings, or enhanced intelligence, or—"

"I said I'm not interested." She stands, plate in hand. "I'll eat in my room."

"Suit yourself," her mother sighs, already turning her attention to her own reflection in the polished silver serving spoon.

Paige escapes up the stairs, careful to avoid the new sculptures her parents have installed. The abstract metal pieces supposedly complement their evolving aesthetic but really make navigating the house a hazardous undertaking. Like everything else in her home, the art isn't chosen for beauty or meaning, but for how well it showcases her parents' status as cutting-edge altereds.

Her bedroom is the only space untouched by their transformation obsession. When she closes the door behind her, the tension in her shoulders eases. Here, surrounded by her books, her sketches, her soccer trophies, and the star-patterned bedspread she's had since she was twelve, she can almost pretend that life is normal.

She sets her plate on her desk and stares out the window,

where twilight is painting the sky in soft purples and blues. Three years ago, this view included her father tending the garden while her mother called out suggestions from the patio. Now, the garden is overgrown, the patio furniture moldering under forgotten tarps. Her parents are too busy taking nanites and attending altered-only parties to care about something as mundane as yard maintenance.

Paige's phone buzzes with a text. Carson.

Still on for tomorrow after school? Treehouse?

She smiles for the first time since coming home.

Absolutely. Need to escape this asylum.

Carson replies immediately. *That bad?*

Worse. College fund down to $2K. Dad spent it on indestructible bones or something.

There's a pause before the next message appears.

Shit, Paige. I'm sorry. We'll figure something out. Promise.

She types back a heart emoji, sets her phone down, and finally starts eating her now-cold dinner. The food tastes like nothing, but she forces it down anyway, knowing she needs strength. For what, she's not entirely sure yet, but a feeling deep in her gut tells her that something has to change. And soon.

From downstairs, she hears the sound of her parents' laughter, followed by the pop of a champagne cork. Another nanite celebration, no doubt. Another step further away from humanity. Another reminder that the people who are supposed to love her unconditionally have chosen self-transformation over their only daughter.

Paige wipes away a tear before it can fall, angry at herself for still being affected after all this time. She should be used to it by now. The neglect, the disappointment, the gradual erasure of her place in their lives.

She glances at her backpack, calculating how much homework she really needs to finish tonight. Instead, she opens her desk drawer and pulls out a small, leather-bound journal. Inside are sketches, notes, and dreams of places far from here. College campuses she's researched, cities she might escape to, lives she might build for herself without the shadow of nanites hanging over her.

Two thousand dollars won't get her far. But it's something. It's a start. And with Carson by her side, the only person who truly sees her, maybe it can be enough.

Tomorrow, in their treehouse sanctuary, they'll make plans. Real ones, this time. Because staying here, watching her parents drift further away from humanity with each new enhancement, is slowly killing her spirit.

And if there's one thing Paige has inherited from her pre-nanite father, it's his determination to survive.

CHAPTER FIVE

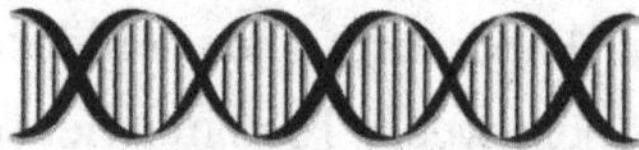

THE TREEHOUSE STANDS like a weathered sentinel among the pines at the edge of the national park, far enough from the walking paths that casual hikers never stumble upon it. From the highest branches, they can see the distant city.

Paige's hands find the familiar notches in the trunk as she climbs, her muscles remembering the way even in the fading light. The wood creaks beneath her weight, a sound that used to terrify her when she was twelve but now feels like a welcome-home whisper. Up here, twenty feet above the ground, there are no nanites, no altered parents with animal features, no President Bear's propaganda videos playing on every screen. Just weathered planks, the lingering scent of Carson's mint gum, and the only person who understands what it means to remain stubbornly, defiantly human in a world racing to become something else.

"Took you long enough," Carson calls down, his toned frame appearing in the square entrance as he extends a hand to help her up the final stretch. "I was starting to think you'd been abducted by those roving enhancement enthusiasts from the mall."

Paige grabs his wrist and pulls herself onto the platform. "Sorry. Mom cornered me on my way out. Wanted to show me her new 'aesthetic palette' for spring." She rolls her eyes, dropping her backpack on the worn rug they'd dragged up here last summer. "Apparently, the shoulder horns are getting iridescent accents next week. To match her scales."

Carson winces. "Your house must look like a zoo crossed with a sci-fi convention by now."

"More like a horror movie," Paige says, settling cross-legged on one of the faded cushions. She takes in the treehouse, their sanctuary since seventh grade. The walls are plastered with polaroids of them at various ages, ticket stubs from concerts, hand-drawn maps of imaginary worlds, and the string lights they installed last year that run on a small solar panel Carson rigged up. In the corner sits their ancient cooler, usually stocked with sodas and snacks.

Carson tosses her a can of cherry cola. "So, two thousand dollars, huh? That's what your college fund is down to." He doesn't phrase it as a question but a confirmation of yesterday's text.

"Yep." Paige cracks open the soda, the fizz a small act of rebellion. Her mother would faint at the sugar content. "Eighteen years of life, and apparently I'm worth exactly two grand to my parents. Less than the cost of Dad's new bone-density nanite."

"That's messed up." Carson leans his head back against the wall.

The treehouse was built when they were kids, and he's

outgrown it more dramatically than she has. At six-foot-two, he's all limbs and angles, his athletic build giving him a grace that serves him well on the lacrosse field. "Have you thought about talking to a guidance counselor? There are scholarships—"

"For unadjusteds?" Paige scoffs. "Name one major university that isn't prioritizing enhanced cognition students now."

Carson's face falls. "You're right. Even Coach Matthews dropped hints that I'd get more play time if I took a speed nanite." He fidgets with the frayed edge of his lacrosse hoodie. "Said all the college scouts are only interested in enhanced players these days."

"You didn't tell me that." Paige studies him, noticing the dark circles under his eyes, the tension in his shoulders. "What did you say?"

"What *could* I say? I told him I'd think about it." Carson stares at his hands. "My dad offered to pay for it as an early graduation present."

Silence settles between them, heavy with understanding. They've had this conversation before. About holding out, staying pure, remaining who they are. But with each passing month, the pressure builds.

"Something else happened, didn't it?" Paige asks, recognizing the tight set of his jaw.

Carson takes a deep breath. "Ryan Kostner and his crew cornered me in the locker room yesterday."

Paige's stomach sinks. Ryan Kostner, lacrosse team captain, son of the school board president, and notorious for his "social purity" crusade. "What did he do?"

"The usual charming homophobic greatest hits." Carson's

laugh is hollow. "But this time, he brought props." He pulls out his phone, pulls up a photo, and passes it to her.

On the screen is Carson's locker covered in printouts of advertisements for the AlignX nanite, the one marketed specifically to "correct sexual orientation anomalies." Someone has drawn crude anatomical illustrations around the edges.

"Oh, Carson." She reaches for his hand.

"It gets better," he says, swiping to the next photo. "They created a fake social media profile using my pictures, claiming I'm looking for the 'cure' because I'm tired of being —" He stops, his voice catching.

"Bastards," Paige whispers.

"The worst part is how many people liked it." Carson takes his phone back, staring at the screen. "Including guys on my team. Guys I thought were friends."

Paige moves closer, leaning her head against his shoulder. For a moment, they just sit there, Carson's breathing gradually slowing as the contact calms him.

"My aunt called my parents last night," he finally says, voice so quiet she barely hears him. "She saw the profile. Thought it was real. She was so...relieved. Told my mom she'd pay for the nanite herself, as a gift."

Paige sits straight with a start. "What did your parents say?"

"They said they'd 'discuss it with me.' Like it's a haircut or something." He closes his eyes. "Dad called it 'a sensible solution to an unnecessary hurdle in life.'"

Paige's anger flares. "That's—"

"Not surprising," Carson finishes for her. "You know how

they are. Image-conscious. Traditional. They love me, but they've never been comfortable with..." He gestures vaguely at himself.

"With you being exactly who you're supposed to be?" Paige says fiercely.

Carson's smile is grim. "Sometimes I wonder if they're right. Not about gay being wrong," he adds quickly, seeing her expression. "But about the nanite being...practical."

"Practical?" She spits out the word.

"Yeah. I mean, look around, Paige. The world isn't exactly evolving in a gay-friendly direction. President Bear's Family Stability Initiative is gaining support. That anti-gay nanite movement is pushing for mandatory normalization for teenagers." He runs a hand through his hair, leaving it standing in messy spikes. "Last week, I read that AlignX prescriptions are up sixty percent from last year."

"That doesn't mean—"

"It means fewer and fewer gay people," Carson says bluntly. "Which means fewer chances to ever meet someone, to fall in love, to have any kind of normal life. Maybe taking the nanite would be easier."

The words hit Paige like a physical blow. "You can't be serious."

"I've been thinking about it," he admits, not meeting her eyes. "What if it's just...simpler? I'm already keeping secrets, pretending to be someone I'm not. At least with the nanite, the pretending would stop. I could date girls. You, even. You're beautiful." He looks at her and chuckles. "I'd make my parents happy, have a future that doesn't involve being a social outcast."

"No." Paige grabs his hands, forcing him to look at her. "No, Carson, that's not you talking. That's them—Ryan, your parents, President Bear, all of them—getting in your head. You can't let them win."

"Is it winning if I'm happier?" His voice cracks. "If I don't have to be afraid anymore?"

"You wouldn't be happier, you'd be someone else entirely." Paige's eyes burn with unshed tears. "That pill wouldn't make you straight, it would erase the real you and replace it with some manufactured version that fits their idea of normal."

Carson pulls his hands away. "You don't know that. Maybe the feelings would be real."

"Like my mother's feelings for her reflection are real?" Paige says. "Like my father's obsession with his next enhancement is real? They're addicted, Carson. The nanites changed more than their bodies. They changed their *souls*."

"This is different," Carson insists.

"How? How is fundamentally altering who you're attracted to not the most invasive change possible?" She takes a deep breath, trying to calm her racing heart. "I've watched my parents vanish nanite by nanite, replaced by these...creatures who care more about their appearances than their own daughter. The real them is gone."

Carson leans forward, elbows on his knees. "But what if there's no future for me the way I am? You've seen the statistics. Gay and lesbian nanite treatments are up, the community is shrinking. Those dating apps my cousin used to use are ghost towns now. Everyone's either going enhanced-straight or into hiding."

"Or fighting back," Paige insists.

"*Fighting back?*" Carson snorts. "Against *what?* The entire government? The pharmaceutical industry? The culture?" He gestures toward the small window that faces the city. "Haven't you see those digiboards advertising nanites that promise to *align your desires with your destiny.* They're all over the place."

Paige looks out the window of the treehouse as if she might be able to see the advertisements from their private sanctuary. She knows the ones Carson is talking about. Sees them every day. Massive digital displays that flash with promises of better bodies, better minds, better lives, all available in convenient pill form. She does her best to ignore them, adopting the ostrich method. But maybe she can't do that anymore.

"Promise me something," she says finally, turning back to him.

"What?"

"Promise you won't make any decisions about this right now. Not while you're hurting, not while Ryan's stupid prank is fresh." She squeezes his shoulder. "Give it time."

Carson hesitates, then nods. "Fine. No decisions yet."

"And one more thing." Paige waits until he meets her eyes. "Promise me you'll never change who you are just to make other people comfortable. Never, Carson. Not for Ryan, not for your parents, not for anyone."

His eyes shimmer with emotion. "That's a harder promise."

"I know. But it's the most important one." She takes his hand again. "What if there was a nanite that could make me want to be like my parents? To want antlers and scales and animal DNA? Would you want me to take it, just to fit in?"

"Of course not," he says immediately. "That wouldn't be you."

"Exactly. And straight Carson wouldn't be you either." Paige smiles gently. "I love you exactly as you are. Stubbornly, gorgeously, authentically you."

A tear slides down his cheek, which he quickly wipes away. "Even if it means being alone forever?"

"You're not alone. You have me." She bumps his shoulder with hers. "Besides, they can't make everyone take those nanites. There have to be others like us out there, people who want to stay human, who reject all this."

"Sometimes I try to imagine what the world would be like without nanites," Carson says softly. "If President Bear had never taken that first regeneration pill for his leg."

"If my dad had found another way to beat cancer," Paige adds.

"We'd still just be...people. Flawed, normal people." Carson's expression grows dreamy. "No antlers in the dinner table chandelier."

Paige laughs despite herself. "No beaks trying to eat spaghetti."

"No venomous government officials with grizzly bear DNA."

They grin at each other, the tension breaking.

"Somewhere," Paige says, "there have to be places where people are resisting all this. Communities of unadjusteds, living real, unaltered lives."

"Like a reservation for the stubbornly human?" Carson muses. "Could be nice."

"Better than nice. Essential." Paige stands, suddenly energized, and paces the small space. "That's where we'll go after high school. We'll find others like us. People who understand that changing your DNA isn't the answer to every problem."

Carson watches her, a smile tugging at his lips. "And how exactly do we find this mythical community?"

"I don't know yet," she admits. "But we will. There have to be others who feel like we do."

The certainty in her voice seems to reach something in Carson. He straightens, looking more like himself than he has all evening.

"Okay," he says. "No nanites. Not for me, not for you. Human and proud, or whatever."

"Exactly." She extends her pinky finger. "Swear it?"

He links his pinky with hers, the childhood gesture still sacred between them. "I swear. No matter what Ryan Kostner does, no matter what my parents say."

"And I swear to never let my parents' obsession become mine," Paige adds. "No matter how alone I feel in that house."

They stay like that for a full minute, fingers linked, a pact between two unadjusteds in a world rushing toward artificial perfection. Outside, the city glows with neon promises of enhancement. But here, in their wooden sanctuary among the trees, they hold onto something more valuable. The freedom to remain exactly who they are.

CHAPTER SIX

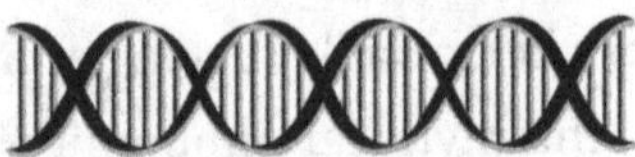

THE SUNSET BLEEDS amber and rose across the horizon, painting the treehouse in warm hues that soften its weathered edges. Paige dangles her legs through the open doorway, watching as shadows lengthen across the park below. She's barely left the treehouse all summer, even eating her meals and doing the pre-reading for the new school year by flashlight. And Carson has been with her for every minute of it.

Carson sits with his back against the frame, knees pulled to his chest, his profile outlined in gold. They've been here for hours, talking, planning, existing in this pocket of time where the world's expectations can't reach them. The distant hum of traffic has faded to a gentle murmur as rush hour ebbs, replaced by the evening chorus of birds settling into their nests. Neither of them mentions how much the birdsong has faded over the years, how the natural world seems to be retreating as the enhanced one expands.

"Zoe Chen took the intelligence nanite yesterday," Carson says, breaking their comfortable silence. "Her parents posted about it on EvolveMe. Called it her 'evolution celebration.'" He absently picks at a splinter stuck in the wooden floor. "That makes five from our old homeroom class this month."

Paige nods, unsurprised but still disappointed. Zoe had been one of the holdouts, a brilliant student who'd often spoken about the value of earning your achievements. "What pushed her over the edge?"

"She wants to go to MIT. Their website 'recommends' cognitive enhancement nanites." Carson makes air quotes with his fingers. "Apparently, the school's entire incoming class is expected to arrive enhanced. They don't explicitly require it, but..."

"But they make it impossible to compete if you don't," Paige finishes. "Classic manipulation."

"According to Eli, who was at the party, she cried after taking it." Carson's voice drops. "Said it felt like her brain was being rewired from the inside out. But an hour later, she was solving quantum physics equations and laughing about how she'd ever struggled with calculus."

Paige shivers despite the warm evening air. "Do you think she's still...her?"

Carson shrugs. "Eli said she seemed the same, just faster. Sharper." He pauses. "Colder, maybe."

They fall silent again, watching the last sliver of sun disappear behind the tree canopy.

"Did you watch the president's speech yesterday?" Paige asks, though she already knows the answer. They've made a pact to stay informed, no matter how disturbing the news becomes.

"Yeah. The 'Evolutionary Imperative' one." Carson's expression darkens. "He was showing off that new venom-web trick. Shot it from his palm and immobilized a volunteer from the audience."

"*Volunteer*," Paige echoes sarcastically. "I'm sure they were thrilled to be publicly cocooned in toxic spider silk."

"The scary part wasn't even the webbing," Carson continues. "It was how the crowd cheered. Like watching their leader display predator abilities was entertainment, not a terrifying abuse of power." He rubs his arms as if suddenly cold. "My dad called it 'magnificent.' Said President Bear is what humanity should aspire to become."

Paige remembers the footage she glimpsed on the living room screen before escaping to her bedroom—President Bear's massive frame, enhanced with grizzly DNA, making him far hairier than the average human. His hands, disproportionately large with curved claws where fingernails should be, gesturing as he spoke about the future. The moment when he demonstrated the enhancement that had earned him three purple hearts during his tours of duty—black widow venom webbing shooting from specialized glands implanted in his palms, encasing a pale, trembling man in sticky strands. The man's face as the venom began to affect his nervous system, his features contorting in pain while the president continued speaking about "necessary evolution."

"He's not human anymore," Paige says quietly. "Not in any way that matters."

"And he's making the rules for all of us." Carson's voice carries a rare edge of bitterness. "His Unadjusted Monitoring Initiative passed the Senate yesterday. Starting next month, anyone who hasn't taken at least one enhancement nanite by age eighteen has to register with the Department of Evolutionary Affairs."

Paige's heart sinks. "Register for what?"

"'Social integration counseling,'" Carson says grimly. "Whatever that means."

"It means they're going to start forcing nanites on people." Paige pulls her legs up from the doorway, suddenly feeling exposed. "First tracking, then 'counseling,' then mandatory 'treatments.' It's already happening with convicted criminals."

"I know." Carson meets her eyes. "And we're stuck in high school with parents who just don't get it."

The implication hangs between them, heavy with urgency. Their time is running out.

"What do we do?" Paige asks.

"What *can* we do?" Carson replies. "We're just kids."

Paige gnaws on her lip, running through the possibilities in her mind. What she'd really like to do is run away. Now. But it's not practical. She's only sixteen. She has no qualifications. If they wait until they both graduate, then maybe they can make a life for themselves somewhere. Somewhere with people just like them.

"We need to leave," Paige says, her thoughts crystallizing. "After high school. We need to that unadjusted community."

Carson doesn't look surprised. "We'll have to register long before then."

"So we leave it as long as we can. Then we register. With both of our parents having enhancements it's not like we're a flight risk." She smirks at her joke. "Then we go somewhere... else." Paige shifts to face him fully. "The northwestern wilderness areas. The abandoned mining towns in Nevada. Somewhere off the grid."

"You're serious." It's not a question.

"Completely." Paige's heart races with a mixture of fear and determination. "Think about it, Carson. Every day we stay here, we're at risk. Your parents are already pushing the sexuality nanite. Mine have burned through my college fund for their enhancements. And now the government wants us registered. What happens when we're officially adults? They'll ram those pills down our throats. Watch my words."

Carson stares out at the darkening sky. "You really think there are places where unadjusteds can still live freely?"

"There have to be." Paige leans forward, energized by the idea. "Remember that news story they tried to bury last year? About the community in the old Olympic Peninsula nature preserve? Before they shut down the reporter's feed, he showed people living normally, growing food, teaching their kids, building homes. No enhancements."

"Until the Nanite Enforcement Unit raided them," Carson reminds her. "Most of them were captured and *rehabilitated*."

"But not all of them," Paige counters. "Some escaped. And there are rumors of other communities—in the mountains, in remote coastal areas, even underground in some of the abandoned subway systems."

Carson considers this. "It would mean giving up everything. College. My lacrosse scholarship possibilities. Your dream of art college."

"You think I want to sketch pretty drawings while the world is going to hell?" Paige gives a hollow laugh. "And with what money? College fund gone, remember? Besides, you heard what happened with Zoe. Even if we got in somewhere, they'd just pressure us to enhance."

"True." Carson pulls his phone from his pocket, taps through a few screens, then shows it to Paige. "I've been researching, too. There's an encrypted forum where people share information about unadjusted-friendly zones."

Paige takes the phone, scanning the messages with growing excitement. Users with code names discussing safe routes, supportive communities, ways to live off the grid. "You've been thinking about this already!"

"Since Ryan's locker decoration project." Carson's smile is tinged with sadness. "I realized I had two choices: take a nanite that would erase who I am or find a place where being me isn't a liability."

"We could do this," Paige whispers, scrolling through more messages. "We really could."

"It won't be easy," Carson warns. "We'll need supplies, transportation, money. A plan for when the initial resources run out. Skills to survive wherever we end up."

"I have two thousand dollars," Paige offers. "It's not much, but it's something."

"I've been saving from my weekend job at the sporting goods store. About three thousand." Carson chews his lip. "And I know how to fish, how to set up camp. My dad used to take me, before he got so enhancement-obsessed."

"I can garden," Paige adds. "And I've been teaching myself basic first aid from those videos online. Plus, I can barter with art. People always need signs, decorations, personalized items."

They look at each other, the possibility taking shape between them.

"We'd have to be careful about communication," Carson says, thinking aloud. "All the standard channels are monitored now. We'd need to plan in person, not digitally."

"The treehouse," Paige suggests. "We meet here, plan everything."

"And we don't tell anyone. Not your parents, not mine. Not a single friend." Carson's expression is deadly serious. "The fewer people who know, the better our chances."

Paige nods, the weight of secrecy already settling on her shoulders. "So we go as soon as we graduate?"

Carson shakes his head. "Before. We spend the next year doing AP classes and getting extra credit, see if we can graduate a year early. Then we run."

One year. She can do that. She can work her ass off and get her diploma in one year.

"Too soon?" Carson asks.

Paige thinks about going home tonight, about facing her mother's beak and her father's antlers, about the empty promises and the dwindling college fund. She thinks about the city's billboards promoting "evolutionary progress" and President Bear's venomous webs. She thinks about Zoe Chen, crying as the nanite rewired her brain.

"Not soon enough."

"We need those qualifications," Carson says. "If we don't have enhancements, no one is going to give two high school dropouts a chance."

"I know," Paige says quietly, trying to ignore the fear gripping the back of her neck. "I just hope it's soon enough."

Carson reaches over and squeezes her hand. "We'd be leaving everything behind. Everyone we know."

"Who do we really have left?" Paige asks softly. "Zoe was my friend since elementary school, and yesterday she took a pill that changed her brain. Eli only talks about his enhanced reflexes now. Madison grew gills last month and spends all her time at the new underwater mall." She shakes her head. "They're not the people we knew anymore."

"I know." Carson's voice is thick with emotion. "Sometimes at practice, I look around and realize I barely recognize anyone. Half the team has taken strength enhancements or speed nanites, or bulked up. Some of them have literal predator DNA mixing with their own." He shivers. "Jackson's eyes glow in the dark now. Actually glow. He says it gives him night-game advantage."

The last light fades from the sky, leaving them in the warm glow of their solar-powered string lights. The tiny bulbs cast starry patterns on the wooden ceiling, a private constellation mapping their future.

"One year," Carson says decisively. "Less than that. School starts next week. So nine months, and we're gone. We head north, following the route from the forum."

"To find others like us," Paige adds. "People who still want to be people."

"It's going to be dangerous," Carson warns.

"Staying would be more dangerous." Paige looks into the dark forest, feeling more at home than anywhere else. "At least this way, we're choosing our path, not having it chosen for us."

They sit in silence for a moment, the enormity of their

decision filling the small space. In the distance, a Bear Administration surveillance drone hums over the park, its sensors sweeping the ground below. They instinctively press back from the doorway, though they know the treehouse is well-hidden among the thick branches.

"Do you think we'll make it?" Carson asks, his voice barely audible over the drone's mechanical whirr.

Paige watches the device move on, its blinking red eye searching for signs of "social deviation"—the government's term for unadjusted gatherings. When it disappears out of sight, she lets a breath.

"We have to," she says simply. "Because the alternative isn't living. It's surrendering everything that makes us who we are."

Carson nods, his determination visibly strengthening. "Nine months," he says. "Nine months to sit tight, and then we find our people."

"Our people," Paige echoes, finding comfort in the phrase. "Somewhere out there."

CHAPTER SEVEN

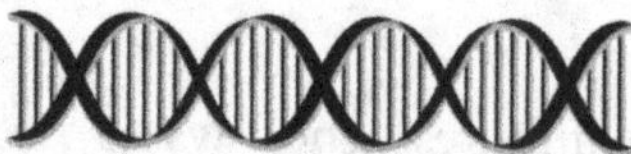

CARSON IS NEVER LATE. Not for the first day of school. Not for anything.

They usually meet at the street corner halfway between their houses and walk on together from there. But it's fifteen minutes past their agreed time and he's not here.

The morning sun filters through the leaves of the old oak tree, casting dappled shadows across the tarmac. Paige checks her watch for the third time in five minutes. She tucks a strand of dark hair behind her ear and peers down the street, scanning the familiar sidewalk where Carson should be coming from. No sign of her best friend's figure jogging toward her. An uneasy feeling settles in her stomach, heavier than the humidity pressing down from the summer sky.

"Come on, Carson," she whispers, drumming her fingers against her thigh. "Where are you?"

Sunlight pounds the back of her neck, already promising a brutally hot day. A bead of sweat drips down her back. A driverless car races down the road, takes the corner at speed.

The digiboard above her head flickers to life, delivering personalized messages. Does she want to be like the rest of her classmates? Did she know that only ten percent of her class remain unadjusted? Doesn't she admire her mother's iridescent scales?

Paige blocks it all out, gnawing on her lip, willing Carson to appear.

"Thirty-seven minutes," she says to no one. "That's not just running late."

Carson has never been more than five minutes late, and even then, he texts. She checks her phone again. No messages. No missed calls. The screen remains stubbornly blank.

Something is wrong.

After another ten minutes, she can't take it anymore. She's already missed homeroom and first period has started. She repositions her backpack and heads down the street toward the Callahan house.

Each block showcases obvious examples of nanite modifications—a woman watering flowers with skin that shifts colors like a living mood ring; a man jogging with legs that extend an extra foot with each stride for maximum efficiency. A group of college guys play basketball on an outdoor court, one guy's arms stretching unnaturally to make an impossible shot.

The division between the adjusteds and unadjusteds grows more visible every day. Paige keeps her head down, aware of how normal she looks. How unenhanced. How natural.

Carson's house sits at the end of Maple Street, a two-story

colonial with a perfectly manicured lawn. Mrs. Callahan prides herself on her garden, all grown naturally. One of the few things she doesn't believe needs improvement.

Paige hesitates at the edge of the driveway. Something feels off. The curtains are drawn, and both cars are parked in front of the garage. Normally both of Carson's parents would be at work by now.

She rings the doorbell and listens to the familiar chime echo inside. Footsteps approach, slow and measured. The door opens a crack, and Mrs. Callahan peers out, her expression tightening when she sees Paige.

"Oh, Paige. Shouldn't you be at school?"

"Hi, Mrs. Callahan. Is Carson here? We were supposed to walk to school together. Like always. But he never showed."

A flicker of something—guilt? fear?—crosses Mrs. Callahan's face. "No, honey, he's not here."

Paige frowns. What isn't she telling her? "Where...where is he? We're already late." Paige tries to keep her voice casual, but her heart hammers against her ribs.

Mrs. Callahan glances over her shoulder, then steps outside, pulling the door almost closed behind her. "Paige, Carson won't be home for a while. He's...he's transferred to a boarding school."

"Transferred?" Her stomach hollows, and the ground rushes up to meet her. Paige places a hand on the door to steady herself. "When? Why? He never told me..." Hot tears prick her eyes. They were going to endure the year together. Study together. Motivate each other so they could graduate at the end of the year. But now...he's gone.

"It was a last-minute decision. A wonderful opportunity," she says lightly, *too* lightly. "A school for boys just like him. To help them...develop properly."

The euphemism hangs in the air between them, and Paige feels the blood drain from her face. "What kind of development?"

Mrs. Callahan lowers her voice. "We found some concerning materials in his room—pictures, messages. Things that suggested he was...confused about certain aspects of himself." She reaches out and pats Paige's shoulder with cold fingers. "It's just a phase, of course, but we thought it best to get him help before it becomes a problem. This school will provide that environment. Among other things."

Paige's throat constricts. "Mrs. Callahan, where exactly is Carson?"

"Bright Future Rehabilitation School. It's got an excellent success rate. The newest nanite therapy, very targeted. He'll be back by Christmas, good as new." She says this with the bright, empty enthusiasm of someone reciting a brochure. "Better, even."

"You gave him a nanite?" Paige whispers, her voice cracking. "Without his consent?"

Mrs. Callahan's expression hardens. "He's sixteen, Paige. We don't need his consent to get him proper medical care. The AlignX nanite is FDA approved and has helped thousands of confused young people find their true path."

The words hit Paige like physical blows. A straight nanite. They're reprogramming his brain, rewriting his identity.

"That's not care," Paige says, her hands curling into fists at her sides. "That's conversion. That's—that's torture."

"I think you should go home now, Paige." Mrs. Callahan steps back toward the door. "Carson will be back at Christmas, and I'm sure he'll be happy to see you then. Though he might have...different interests by that point."

"Can I at least talk to him? Call him or something?"

"No outside contact for the first month. It interferes with the adjustment process." Mrs. Callahan's tone suggests this conversation is over. "I'll tell him you stopped by when we're allowed to speak with him."

Before Paige can protest further, the door closes firmly in her face. She stands there, stunned, tears building behind her eyes. Carson is gone. Taken away to have his brain chemically altered because his parents can't accept who he is.

She stumbles back down the driveway, bile rising in her throat. Her vision blurs as she walks, barely registering her surroundings. All she can think about is Carson. Gentle, thoughtful Carson who stayed up all night talking her through her panic attacks when her parents first started changing, who never judged her for being unadjusted, who trusted her with his deepest secret.

Now that secret has been discovered—and deemed a problem to be fixed with nanite technology. The same technology that stole her parents from her, that's creating artificial divides in society, is being used to erase a fundamental part of her best friend.

Paige finds herself at the treehouse without consciously deciding it. She climbs the ladder with leaden limbs and collapses onto the floor, hugging her knees to her chest.

Their plans lie in ruins. All of it meaningless now. When he returns, he won't be the same. What if he becomes not just straight, but pro nanite? What if he's taken more by the time she sees him?

A heaviness fills Paige's body. No matter how he returns, she knows she's lost her best friend.

What's the point in running now? She can't do it on her own. She's not strong enough. She needs her friend.

"I should have protected you somehow," she whispers to the empty treehouse. "I should have seen this coming."

But how could she have? Carson was always so careful. Someone must have gone through his things, invaded his privacy. The thought makes her anger flare, hot and sudden, burning away some of the initial shock.

Paige sits up, wiping tears from her cheeks with the back of her hand. She can't help Carson if she falls apart. She needs to think. To plan. Maybe there's a way to reach him, to remind him of who he really is before the nanites completely rewrite his brain chemistry.

The unadjusted underground network might know something about the Bright Future School. They might have resources, information that could help. But approaching them alone, without Carson by her side, feels overwhelming. He was always the brave one, the one with connections and plans.

Now she's on her own. Junior year stretches before her like an endless, empty road. No Carson. No parents who care enough to notice she's falling apart. Just Paige, staring at her lost reflection in the treehouse window, more alone than she's ever been.

CHAPTER EIGHT

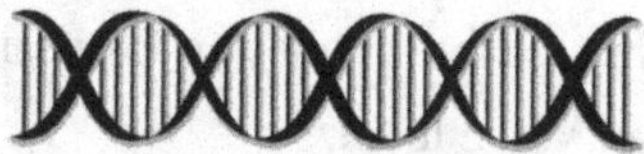

PAIGE STANDS in the doorway of her parents' bedroom, arms crossed, watching as they toss designer clothes into their matching leather suitcases. Her mother holds up two dresses with feather-textured sleeves—a modification from her last nanite—and squints at them through cat-slit pupils that glow faintly in the dimmed light. Her father doesn't even look up, too busy admiring how the bioluminescent antlers sprouting from his temples pulse in sync with his heartbeat. Neither of them notices Paige's reflection in the mirror, a normal human girl fading into the background of her own home.

"So you're really going," she says, her voice cutting through their chatter about packing lists and cruise excursions.

Her mother turns, blinking those unnatural, feline eyes. "Paige! Didn't see you there, sweetie. Yes, we're just finishing up. The car service arrives in an hour."

"Three months." Paige steps into the room, fingers digging into her arms. "You'll be gone for three months."

"It's the opportunity of a lifetime," her father says, not bothering to face her. The necklace implant embedded in his throat flashes with each word. "A world cruise designed specifically for the enhanced. There's a whole program of body modification ceremonies in international waters. Things you can't get in the States yet."

"You do realize I'll be alone for Christmas?" Paige asks, fighting to keep her voice level.

Her mother waves a dismissive hand, her blue shoulder horns catching the light. "You don't want to spend Christmas with your folks anymore, honey. Mrs. Callahan already said you could join them for Carson's big homecoming. And we'll call you from the ship!"

"Right. Sure. Okay. Whatever." The bitterness in her throat is thick enough to choke on.

For a moment, silence falls over the room. Her father finally turns, his expression somewhere between annoyance and confusion. "Paige, you're old enough to understand that adults have lives too. This cruise is important for our social connections. Half the city's elite will be there. The networking alone—"

"Is more important than me. Got it." Paige nods, the familiar hurt turning to numbness. "I've understood that since the first nanite."

Her mother sighs dramatically. "Not this again. We've left you plenty of money for food and emergencies. It's all in your bank account."

"Whatever. I'll be in my room," she says. "Don't bother saying goodbye."

She walks out before they can respond, though she doubts they would.

An hour later, she hears the front door close, followed by the sound of rolling luggage on the driveway and car doors slamming. The house falls silent. Paige sits on her bed, staring at her banking app on her phone. Two hundred dollars. The pitiful remainder of what was supposed to be her future. The rest has been spent on her parents' transformations, their new social lives, their endless quest for the next modification that will make them feel special.

She clicks into her recent calls. She's tried calling the Bright Future Rehabilitation School countless times, only to be told that Carson can't receive calls during his adjustment period. She's tried emailing him, texting him, even sending an actual letter. Nothing gets through.

The emptiness of the house presses in on her, a physical weight on her chest. Three months of this. Three months of silence and abandonment. Christmas is two weeks away. She doesn't go to the parties over the break. Too many wings and feathers and beaks and antlers and glow in the dark skin that it all gives her a headache. Carson doesn't come home. Apparently the first treatment didn't take so he has to stay longer. Paige spends Christmas alone.

She doesn't bother putting up the tree. Doesn't bother cooking a fancy meal—she doesn't want to waste the money on the ingredients. She doesn't even buy herself a present. She stares at the dollar figure in her back account again. Useless for college now. She could save it, be practical. Or she could use it to survive in a different way.

The thought that has been circling the edges of her mind for days finally lands, fully formed: a nanite. Not to become like her parents—never that—but something that might make them notice her again. Something that might help her feel less alone.

Carson would tell her not to do it. He'd remind her of their pact to stay natural, to resist the pressure. But Carson isn't here. Carson is having his brain chemistry rewritten against his will, and no one seems to care.

Paige powers up her laptop and navigates to an encrypted browser. The black market isn't hard to find if you know where to look, and Carson—ironically—had shown her months ago, part of their research into underground resistance movements.

She finds an address in the industrial district, memorizes it, then deletes her browser history. For a moment, she hesitates, staring at her reflection in the black laptop screen. What would the old Paige say about what she's about to do? The Paige from before her parents started changing, before Carson was taken away?

She doesn't know that girl anymore.

After she drains the money in her bank, she walks the hour journey into the city. The sun is setting, painting the abandoned warehouses in shades of orange and red.

Paige pulls her hoodie closer, keeping her head down as she navigates streets that grow progressively emptier of legitimate businesses and fuller of shadowy figures conducting transactions in doorways.

The black market itself is hidden inside what appears to be a condemned textile factory. Paige approaches slowly, her heart hammering as she spots the subtle marking beside the side entrance—a small DNA helix spray-painted in iridescent paint, visible only from certain angles.

Even though it's Christmas Day, a man leans against the wall beside the door, tall and broad-shouldered, his face obscured by a hood. As Paige approaches, he tilts his head slightly.

"Lost, little girl?" His voice is surprisingly gentle.

"No." She straightens her shoulders. "I'm looking to make a purchase."

"Lotta things for sale around here. Some legal, some not."

"I'm not a cop."

He chuckles. "Didn't think you were. Cops send in older undercovers." He studies her for a moment. "First time?"

She nods, trying to look more confident than she feels.

"Word of advice," he says, stepping away from the wall. "Don't look scared, don't look eager. Don't haggle unless you know the real price. And don't take anything without seeing the certification code first, even if it costs extra. Too many counterfeits floating around." He opens the door, gesturing for her to enter. "Good luck."

The interior of the factory has been transformed into a sprawling marketplace. Strings of lights hang from exposed rafters, illuminating rows of booths and tables. People of all descriptions wander between them, some obviously enhanced, others appearing natural but likely hiding modifications beneath clothing. The air smells of sweat, metal, and something chemical that burns the back of Paige's throat.

Many people wear Christmas sweaters, cash clenched in their fists, ready to spend. Is this how people spend the holidays now?

She moves through the crowd, scanning signs and displays. There are booths selling everything from basic cosmetic nanites to military-grade enhancements that are definitely illegal. Some vendors display their wares openly. Others whisper to clients, sliding catalogs or samples from beneath counters.

Paige approaches a booth with a flickering holographic sign that reads "Certified Nanites - All Effects Guaranteed." The guy behind the counter has skin that shimmers with a metallic gleam, and his eyes shift color continuously, cycling through the rainbow.

"Can I help you?" he asks, his gaze assessing Paige with practiced ease. He's only a few years older than her. Recognition dawns. He went to her high school, graduated three years ago. Ryker something.

"I'm looking for something..." Paige hesitates. What exactly is she looking for? Something to make her visible? Something to help her survive the loneliness? "Something that will make people notice me. But not...not too extreme."

Ryker smiles, revealing teeth that appear to be made of tiny diamonds. "First enhancement, huh? I've got some nice starter packages. Subtle glow effects, minor physical alterations, personality boosters—"

"How much?" Paige interrupts.

"Depends on what you want. Basic eye color shifts start at five hundred. Skin textures, one thousand. Anything structural—bone modifications, additional appendages—that's two thousand minimum."

Paige's stomach twists. She doesn't have that much.

"What can I get for two hundred?" She's almost embarrassed to say it.

Ryker shoots her a sympathetic look. "To be honest, not much. Inflation has skyrocketed. Even a permanent tan nanite is more than that now. But..." He reaches beneath the counter and pulls out a small box. "I do have lucky dip nanites. Random effects, certified safe, but you don't know what you'll get until it happens. Two hundred even."

"Random?" Paige frowns. "How random? I don't want to end up with something...harmful."

"All our nanites are FDA regulation-adjacent," Ryker says with a smirk. "These won't kill you or cause permanent damage to vital systems. They're mostly returned stock or excess inventory repackaged. Could be anything from minor cosmetic changes to major structural modifications. Some people love the surprise element."

Or the plausible deniability, Paige thinks. If she doesn't choose a specific modification, is she really betraying her principles? Is she really becoming like her parents?

"Let me see the certification," she says, remembering the doorman's advice.

Ryker turns the box over, revealing a holographic seal with a QR code. Paige scans it with her phone, and sure enough, a verification page appears, confirming the nanite's manufacturing source and safety testing.

"Legitimate product, mystery results," he says. "Two hundred. One time offer for anyone from Northpoint High."

Paige flushes. "You remember me?"

Ryker nods. "You got nice eyes."

Paige's fingers close around the money in her pocket. This is it. Her last chance to walk away, to stay true to the principles she and Carson swore to uphold. But what good did those principles do Carson? What good are they doing her now, alone in an empty house, forgotten by everyone who should care about her?

"I'll take it," she says, placing the cash on the counter.

"Welcome to the new world." Ryker takes the money, then slides the small box across to Paige. "Enjoy your transformation. No refunds, no complaints."

Paige tucks the box into her jacket pocket and turns away, her heart racing. She's just spent her entire future on a chance, a random roll of the genetic dice. She weaves through the crowded market, past dealers hawking nanites that promise everything from eternal youth to superhuman strength, past customers eager to become anything but themselves.

Outside, the night air cools her flushed skin. The same doorman nods to her as she passes.

"Find what you were looking for?" he asks.

Paige touches the box in her pocket. "I don't know yet."

The journey home passes in a blur. As she walks through the streets lit with Christmas lights, she keeps her hand on the nanite box, feeling its edges through the fabric of her jacket. She doesn't want to go home. There is nothing for her there. Instead, she heads to the treehouse as resolution sets deep in her bones.

Her parents chose nanites over her. The world took Carson away and forced a nanite on him.

Maybe it's time she chose for herself, before someone else chooses for her.

CHAPTER NINE

THE NANITE PILL sits in the center of Paige's palm, smaller than she expected. Just a white capsule with faint iridescent swirls beneath its surface. Nothing to hint at the chaos it contains, at the genetic code that will rewrite her body in ways she can't predict. She sits cross-legged on a cushion in the treehouse, the rustle of the leaves her only companion, moonlight streaming through the window.

There is no one to stop her. No one to care. Her thumb traces the smooth surface of the pill. Whatever happens next, it's her choice. The first real choice she's made in years.

"Here goes everything," she whispers, raising the pill to her lips.

She hesitates for one final moment. Carson's face flashes in her mind—his disappointed expression, the betrayal in his eyes if he could see her now. But the Carson she knows is gone, being rewritten by force. At least her transformation is by choice.

Paige swallows the pill with a can of cherry soda. For a moment, nothing happens. She waits, hands trembling, wondering if she's been scammed. Two hundred dollars for a sugar pill would be just her luck.

Then it begins. Warmth spreads from her stomach, like drinking hot tea on a cold day. Pleasant at first, then increasingly intense. Her skin tingles, every nerve ending suddenly awake and alert. She pulls off her sweatshirt, leaving just a tank top as her body temperature rises.

"Okay," she breathes, trying to stay calm. "This is normal. This is supposed to happen."

The warmth sharpens into heat, then intensifies into a burning sensation between her shoulder blades. Paige gasps, arching her back as sharp pain lances down her spine. She stumbles to the small window, twisting to glimpse her reflection. Beneath the thin fabric of her tank top, her skin ripples, stretching—something pushing from underneath.

"Oh god," she whispers, fear mixing with fascination.

The pain intensifies, and she bites down on her fist to keep from crying out. Her back is splitting open from the inside. She falls to her knees, breathing in short, sharp gasps as the nanites do their work, rewriting her DNA, restructuring bone and muscle and skin.

Something rips. The back of her tank top tearing as two small protrusions push through her skin. Blood trickles down her spine, but as she watches in the window, the wounds knit shut, the nanites accelerating her healing as they continue their transformation.

The protrusions lengthen, extending outward, sheathed in a thin, translucent membrane that gradually darkens as it takes shape. Feathers. Tiny at first, then growing, unfurling like plants seeking sun. Emerald green, the exact shade of her eyes, with hints of pine and teal near the edges.

Paige watches, transfixed, as wings unfold from her back. Wings. *Holy shit!* She wasn't expecting anything like this. Normally wings cost thousands.

The pain subsides to a dull ache, then to a strange pressure as the new appendages continue to develop. She feels new muscles forming, neural pathways connecting to her brain, her body adapting to accommodate this dramatic change.

It takes nearly an hour for the transformation to complete. When it's finally done, Paige stands shakily, staring at her new appendages in wonderment. The wings extend from just below her shoulder blades, folded against her back but still reaching down past her waist. They're massive, each wing nearly the length of her arm when folded.

"Wings," she whispers, reaching back to touch them hesitantly. The feathers are soft but strong, vibrant emerald with the complex patterning of macaw plumage.

She tries to move them, focusing on these new muscles she never had before. At first, nothing happens. Then, with a sudden snap that makes her jump, the wings unfurl partially, tearing a picture of her and Carson that was taped to the wall.

"Crap!" Paige scrambles to pick it up the torn photo, the wings moving unpredictably with her motions, bumping against the walls. She needs space. Somewhere to learn how to control these new appendages without destroying the treehouse.

She creeps onto the small ledge that overlooks the forest. Twenty feet up. She gulps. Swallows her fear. There's no point having wings unless she can use them to fly.

But everything feels different—her balance, her weight distribution, even the way air currents move around her body.

She focuses on the new muscles in her back, trying to establish control. Slowly, intentionally, she extends her wings to their full span. The movement sends a thrill through her body as the wings stretch out, revealing their true size. Easily twelve feet from tip to tip. The moonlight catches the green feathers, making them shimmer with iridescent highlights.

"Holy shit," she breathes, amazed at the sheer beauty of what's happened to her. Whatever else nanites have done to the world, to her family, she can't deny the strange perfection of these wings. How they match her eyes exactly, how they seem to belong to her body as though they were always meant to be there.

As she holds onto the wall of the treehouse, she practices opening and closing them, learning the nuances of control. It's like learning to walk again, developing muscle memory for limbs that didn't exist hours ago. After several minutes of practice, the wings begin to respond more naturally to her thoughts, moving with growing precision.

Paige looks up at the night sky, stars visible through breaks in the clouds. She can't put off this moment anymore. She leaps off the ledge.

For a terrifying moment, she drops like a stone. Then instinct—or nanites—kicks in. Her wings catch the air, transforming the fall into a glide. She soars across the clearing, feet skimming the tops of the leaves and pinecones, before the ground rises to meet her and she tumbles into an ungraceful landing.

Paige laughs, picking herself up and brushing grass from her knees. Not quite flying, but definitely not falling either. She climbs the ladder again, determined to get it right.

On her fourth attempt, it happens. She jumps, extends her wings, and instead of just gliding, she flaps. Powerful, rhythmic strokes that generate enough lift to keep her airborne. She rises, wobbling at first, then stabilizing as she finds the right pattern of movement.

"I'm flying," she gasps, her voice caught by the wind. "I'm actually flying!"

Twenty feet above the ground, then thirty, then fifty—she circles the forest, each wingbeat becoming more confident than the last. The sensation is unlike anything she's ever experienced, a perfect combination of effort and effortlessness, of control and surrender. She banks left, then right, testing her maneuverability, learning how subtle shifts in her wing position affect her direction.

Paige climbs higher, riding an updraft that carries her above the treetops. From here, she can see home, the empty streets, the distant glow of the city center. The world looks different from above. Smaller and larger at the same time, more connected, less confined by artificial boundaries.

Her neighborhood spreads out below her, the houses reduced to dark shapes with glowing windows. The night air is cool against her face, rushing through her hair. She can feel every current, every thermal, the nanites having enhanced not just her body but her perception of the air itself.

She flies for what feels like hours but might be minutes,

time losing meaning in the pure joy of movement. When exhaustion finally begins to set in, the new muscles protesting their extended first use, she circles back to her yard, executing a somewhat clumsy but successful landing on the lawn.

Paige collapses onto the grass, wings sprawled wide, breathing hard. The sky above is beginning to lighten with the first hints of dawn. She's been flying all night without realizing it, lost in the freedom of the air.

Her body aches pleasantly, the kind of soreness that comes from discovering new capabilities. The wings, now resting against the cool grass, feel as natural as her arms or legs. Not an addition but an extension of who she always was.

In the growing light, she examines the feathers more closely. The emerald green exactly matches her eyes, with subtle variations in shade creating depth and dimension. Near the edges, hints of pine and teal catch the light. They're beautiful. Objectively, undeniably beautiful.

Is this how it started for her parents? This feeling of wonder at what their bodies could become? For the first time, Paige feels a flicker of understanding for their obsession. The transformation is intoxicating, the new possibilities exhilarating.

But there's a difference, she thinks. Her parents changed to fit in, to follow trends, to be noticed by others. Their modifications became substitutes for personality, for connection, for genuine human experience. They changed to become someone else.

Paige touches her wings gently, feeling the soft feathers beneath her fingertips. She hasn't changed to become someone else. Somehow, impossibly, she feels more herself than ever. The wings haven't replaced something, they've revealed something that was always there. A desire for freedom. For escape. For seeing the world from a different perspective.

She sits up, folding the wings against her back, marveling at how naturally they settle into position. What will her parents think when they return from their cruise? Will they finally notice her? Will they appreciate the irony that their neglect drove her to the very technology they worship?

Does she even care anymore?

Paige stretches her wings out one more time in the morning light, watching how they catch the sun's rays. Whatever comes next, whether her parents notice her or not, whether society accepts her or rejects her, she has this. This power. This freedom. This choice she has made for herself.

And somewhere, in a rehabilitation school with its cold halls and carefully controlled environments, Carson is having his identity stripped away against his will. The contrast isn't lost on Paige. Her transformation didn't just give her wings, it gave her clarity.

She stands, her decision made. She won't wait for her parents to return. Won't sit in this empty house for three months. There are others out there, the unadjusted underground, the resistance groups she and Carson researched. People fighting against forced modifications, against the pressure to change for someone else's comfort.

With her wings, she can find them. With her story, she might help them. And maybe, somehow, she can find a way to help Carson too.

Paige looks to the brightening sky, her wings twitching with anticipation. This isn't the end of her story. It's barely the beginning. She spreads her wings wide, the wind lifting her feathers, and leaps—soaring into the morning light, finally, gloriously free.

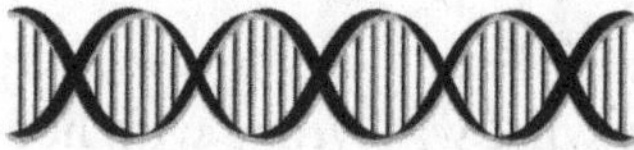

HER PARENTS never called on Christmas Day. They haven't read a single one of her messages either. No response to the photos of green wings.

Mom: *Look what happened to me!*

[*Image attached: Paige, tears streaking her face, newly sprouted wing buds tearing through her T-shirt*]

Dad: *I did this for you. For US. Please come home.*

[*Image attached: Full green wings, half-extended*]

Mom & Dad: *I don't know where you are, but I'm leaving. I'm finding people who will see me.* [*Image attached: Paige's face, determined, wings fully extended behind her*]

And when they return in the middle of March, they pat her head and tell her they're glad she's doing her bit to keep up with the family. Then go about their usual routine. Which is, for the most part, ignoring her.

Carson didn't come home. His mom said he would probably finish high school there. He's not allowed communication with his old friends, not while his transition is so delicate.

When she went back to school after Christmas break, she was asked to join the cheerleading team. Nope. She was invited to the altereds-only after school club. Nope. She was asked to run for class president in senior year. Nope. She was asked to enter the Altered beauty pageant. Nope. She was asked to join the skyball team.

Nope. Nope. Nope.

She was asked what was wrong with her.

Do kindly *fuck off*.

Then they left her alone.

She didn't graduate at the end of her junior year. She missed too much school mourning Carson's absence. She wanted to get away, but with her now being registered and enhanced, there wasn't an immediate rush. It gave her more time to contact the unadjusted underground network. To make friends. To hatch plans. Bigger plans than what Carson and her had been planning.

She was debating whether to bother going to prom and her graduation ceremony when President Bear's announcement came during school hours, right before the first bell rang. She was the only one in class with Mrs. Voss when the tannoy system went into overdrive. As instructed, Mrs. Voss flicked on the screen at the front of the class.

"...breaking news from the White House," the anchor's voice into the classroom. *"President Bear is addressing the nation with what his office calls a 'significant public safety announcement."*

Mrs. Voss raises her eyebrows and increases the volume. A couple more kids wander into the room. She sees Eli, her and Carson's old friend. *New friend again*, Paige realizes, *since she's had her wings.*

The screen changes to show President Bear standing at a podium, his massive frame hardly contained by his tailored suit. The bear-like features grafted onto his otherwise human face, the result of his much-publicized grizzly nanite enhancement, catch the light as he leans toward the microphone.

"This is a national announcement." His voice vibrates with authority that seems to reach through the TV's speakers and grip the inside of Paige's chest. *"All unadjusteds age twelve and over will now be required to take a nanite pill to enhance their abilities. With threats and competition from overseas, we must do more to further the strength of our country."*

The thought crashes into Paige's brain with the force of a speeding train. Required? All unadjusteds? The words echo in her mind, each iteration growing louder, more insistent. Her fingernails dig into her palms as she fights to keep her breathing steady, to not draw attention to herself.

Beside her, Mrs. Voss inhales sharply. "They're making it mandatory now," she whispers.

Mrs. Voss appears unadjusted. There's nothing showy about her. But of course, she may have taken an invisible nanite. Increased cognition, speed, swirling tattoos under her silk blouse...hell, she could have a class ten and be able to teleport. Although what use that would do in a classroom, Paige isn't sure.

As President Bear continues, Paige finds herself leaning closer, straining to hear every word. The president's red eyes gleam with an emotion Paige can't quite identify. Triumph? Anticipation?

"The nanite representative agency is on its way to every school right now." His second declaration comes with a wave of his massive hand, as if physically directing his forces across the country. *"They will assign each eligible unadjusted a ticket number. You are not permitted to leave before you have your ticket. This ticket will tell you which day within the next two weeks you will be assessed for an appropriate nanite level. You'll notice some of those assessments start today. Nanite reps and soldiers are on their way to each school in every city to aid the process..."*

A murmur ripples through the gathering students behind her.

A kid with small horns scans the screen. "About time," he says to no one in particular, loud enough for his voice to carry. "This country needs strength, not weakness."

An unadjusted girl flinches as if she's been slapped, but remains mute. This is not the time for the unadjusteds to speak out.

Eli pumps an enhanced bicep. "Everyone needs to remember I'm the original bulk in this school!"

His statement is met with laughter. *Laughter.*

Paige meets Mrs. Voss gaze.

"It should be a choice," Paige whispers.

The unadjusted girl runs from the classroom. Paige goes after her to try and get her to calm down, to act smart. But by the time Paige exits the room, the girl is already at the front doors. And there are five big bulks dressed in military uniform ready with tasers.

She goes down. Paige swallows an involuntary scream.

Classroom doors open and shut. People fill the hallways. With tears in her eyes, Paige slips out the front door.

No. She will have no part of this. It's time to run. To fly.

A few minutes later, Paige bursts through her front door and dashes up the stairs. She moves methodically around her room, pulling open drawers and filling a backpack with what she'll need. Clothes that accommodate her wings, shirts she's cut open in the back and fitted with buttons, a specially altered jacket. Toiletries. The cash she's been saving. A small photo from before, her parents flanking her at her fourteenth birthday, all of them laughing, all of them still fully human.

She pauses, considers leaving the photo behind, then tucks it into a side pocket. Not to remember what she's lost, but to remember why she's angry.

More details about the closest unadjusted hideout came to her through whispers and fragments. A girl in her bio class with a cousin who escaped the mandatory military enhancement sweeps. A message board frequented by those who are anti-modification. A map sketched hastily on a bathroom stall door before it was painted over by school maintenance. Somewhere in the northern woods, a cave system. Ask for Matt or Francesca. The words "We see you as you are" scrawled like a promise.

Paige zips up her backpack and slides her arms through the straps, adjusting them over her wings. One last action before she goes. She raises her phone, switches to the camera, and takes a photo of herself. Wings extended, backpack on, eyes hard with determination.

She sends it to her parents with a final message: "By the

time you see this, I'll be gone. I found people who don't need to change to be worth something. Don't try to find me."

Her thumb hovers over the send button. The memories flood back unbidden—her father teaching her to ride a bike, his strong hands steady on the seat as she wobbled down the sidewalk. Her mother braiding her hair before school, humming softly as she worked. Family dinners where they talked and laughed and existed in the same space without needing to be more than they were.

That was before cancer stole her father. Before the regeneration nanite that saved him also awakened a hunger for more, for better, for beyond human. Before her mother, terrified of becoming the ordinary one, followed him down that gleaming silver path.

Paige hits send and watches the message status change to "Delivered." She closes her eyes. What if they answer now? What if this is the message that finally breaks through?

One minute passes. Two.

Nothing.

The house feels too empty, too full of ghosts. Paige moves to her bedroom window and pushes it open. Air rushes in, hot against her face. She's practiced flying every day since the modification took and she's now confident she can fly for longer than she can walk. And she can cover more ground too once she takes the bus to the end of the line.

Her wings are strong, but her confidence isn't.

But Matt and the others, the unadjusteds hiding in the caves, they'll help her. They'll see her. They'll tell her what to do. Even with the wings, she's more unadjusted in spirit than adjusted. And it's a place for everyone, no matter who they are, no matter what they look like. She didn't choose enhancement for enhancement's sake; she chose it as a desperate cry for attention. In that way, maybe she's the most human of all.

Paige climbs onto the windowsill. The ground looks far away, the streets bustling with soldiers. But she can't stay a minute longer.

"Okay," she whispers to herself, spreading her magnificent green wings. "You don't need them to see you anymore."

She takes a deep breath, closes her eyes, and jumps. Her wings catch the air, the muscles in her back straining, then stabilizing. She hovers outside her childhood home, a green shadow against the sun.

Then Paige banks left, heading toward the bus station on the edge of town. Flying all the way to the northern woods would be too exhausting, and she doesn't want to draw attention either. The bus will take her most of the way, and then she'll continue on foot or wing, following the fragments of directions she's collected.

She flies over busy streets. Altereds fighting each other, gunning each other down, stabbing each other right through the heart, or the neck, or the back of the leg. Unadjusteds running. Bulk soldiers collaring them all, herding them onto buses with the ominous location tag set as "Northern Compound."

She thinks of Carson and her heart squeezes. *Please be safe*.

When she arrives at the bus station, it smells like artificial pine and fear, a curdling mixture of scents. The bus arrives a few minutes later and Paige makes her way toward the back. She hunches in her seat, wings tucked tight so as not to disturb the other passengers. She passes the day like this, then changes at midnight to a second bus. There are soldiers here, asking them questions, where they are going. But they take one look at her wings and let her on.

The vehicle is half empty. A teenager with skin that glitters like crushed diamonds dozes near the front, his head lolling against the window. An older man with what appears to a single spike protruding from his head scrolls through his phone. Two college-aged girls whisper together, one with normal features, the other sporting electric blue hair that conducts small sparks of electricity when she laughs.

Adjusted and unadjusted, coexisting in uneasy proximity. For now.

The bus rumbles through the city, a steel coffin on wheels, its passengers silent, nervous.

Paige keeps her head down, gaze locked on the blurred neon of passing storefronts. *Don't look interested. Don't look afraid.*

"Can't sleep, dear?"

An older woman across the aisle offers a smile that crinkles the skin around her eyes. Completely natural wrinkles. No nanite-induced agelessness there. The woman's hands, spotted with age, cradle a phone whose glow illuminates her face in harsh blue light.

"No, ma'am," Paige says, her voice quiet, measured. "Long day."

Long life, she thinks but doesn't say.

The woman nods, understanding in her eyes. "Where are you headed?"

"North," Paige answers. Vague enough to be truthful.

Away from parents who transformed themselves into something unrecognizable. Away from the house that became a museum of their vanity.

The woman turns back to her phone, and Paige's attention drifts to the screen. A news anchor with perfect teeth—too perfect, definitely enhanced—speaks with practiced gravity. The volume is low, but Paige catches words that send ice through her veins.

"...unadjusteds being relocated to specialized compounds for their own protection..."

Paige leans closer, pretending to look out the window while her ears strain to catch every word.

"The President's office today announced the implementation of the Protection and Safety Act, authorizing the Nanite Enforcement Agency to establish specialized living facilities for citizens who are genetically unadjusted," the anchor continues. *"Officials stress that these measures are temporary and designed to prevent violence between adjusted and unadjusted populations following yesterday's nanite enforcement announcement."*

The woman notices Paige's interest and tilts the phone slightly toward her. "Terrible business, isn't it?" she whispers. "My grandson is unadjusted. He believes in natural living. I worry about him now."

Paige nods, not trusting herself to speak. The irony doesn't escape her. She sits here with artificial wings grafted to her back, yet would be considered an ally by the unadjusteds simply because she opposes mandatory enhancements. One black market nanite to get her parents' attention, and now she's caught between worlds, belonging to neither.

The news report shifts to show footage of NEA officers in black uniforms escorting people onto buses.

"In related news," the anchor continues, *"the government has announced a reward for information leading to the capture of Dr. Rufus Melody and his daughter, Silver Melody. One million dollars each."*

The screen fills with their images. Dr. Melody with his intelligent eyes and serious expression, Silver with her striking silver eyes that gave her her name. Paige has seen his face countless times in the past few months as the nanite program has grown. He was the creator of the nanite pill. And now he's on the run. Maybe he's just like her.

"The Melodys are wanted in connection with acts of terrorism and for spreading dangerous misinformation about the nanite program," the anchor states. *"Dr. Melody, along with his wife Dr. Margaret Melody who is currently serving a life sentence for treason, was one of the original creators of nanite technology before allegedly sabotaging the program."*

"Poor girl," the woman beside Paige mutters, eyes on Silver's image. "Imagine being hunted like that at her age."

Paige says nothing, but her thoughts race. The Melodys' story fascinated her even before she ran away. They are the scientists responsible for curing her father. They are also responsible for the world falling apart. They may have turned their back on it, but the ball was already in motion. Their names were thrown around in the encrypted resistance chats she'd joined. Whispers of a cure.

The older woman switches off her phone, plunging their section of the bus into relative darkness. "Best not to dwell on such things before trying to sleep," she says, stuffing the device into her purse. "World's gone mad enough without carrying it into our dreams."

Within minutes, soft snores indicate the woman has found the sleep that eludes Paige. The bus continues its journey through the night, headlights cutting through darkness, wheels eating miles of empty highway.

Paige leans her forehead against the cool window glass and lets her mind wander. An hour crawls by. She drifts in and out of a light doze, never fully surrendering to sleep. The prickling sense of unease keeps her alert, a background hum of anxiety that spikes when the bus suddenly slows and pulls to the shoulder of the highway.

The driver's voice crackles over the intercom: "Ladies and gentlemen, we apologize for the interruption. The Nanite Enforcement Agency has established a checkpoint ahead. Please have identification ready."

Murmurs ripple through the previously quiet bus. Passengers rustle through bags and pockets for ID cards. Paige's heart hammers against her ribs as she fumbles for her wallet. Her ID is real, but it doesn't show her enhancement. When she obtained her wings, she never registered them. Black market nanites don't come with paperwork.

The bus doors hiss open. Three NEA officers board, their black uniforms pristine even at this late hour. Two carry handheld scanners; the third, a tablet. They all have guns. Their faces reveal nothing as they begin moving down the aisle.

"Routine check," the one with the tablet announces. "Nothing to worry about if you've got nothing to hide."

The words hang in the air like a threat. Paige watches as

they scan the first few rows of passengers. The device emits a soft beep and displays information only the officers can see.

"What exactly are you looking for?" someone calls from the back.

"Unadjusted citizens who need to be relocated for their protection," the officer replies without looking up. "And unregistered or illegal enhancements."

Shit.

Beside her, the older woman wakes, confusion clouding her face before understanding dawns. "Oh my," she whispers, clutching her purse tighter. "I was hoping to make it to my daughter's before this started happening."

The officers work methodically down the aisle. When they reach a middle-aged man five rows ahead, the scanner emits a different tone. The officers exchange glances.

"Sir, please gather your belongings," one says. "You'll need to come with us."

"What? Why?" The man stands, indignant. "I've done nothing wrong."

"You're classified as unadjusted, sir. For your safety, you're being transferred to a secure facility."

"You mean a camp," the man spits. "This is discrimination!"

Despite his protests, two officers escort him off the bus. Through the windows, Paige watches as he's guided to another vehicle idling on the shoulder. A white bus with tinted windows and the NEA logo emblazoned on its side.

The process repeats: A young woman, an elderly couple, a teenager who can't be more than sixteen. All unadjusted, all removed. With each extraction, the remaining passengers grow quieter, tension thickening the air.

Paige calculates her options, each more desperate than the last. Stay and be discovered for an unregistered enhancement or suspected unadjusted sympathies, it hardly matters which. Or run. But where? They're on an elevated highway section with steep embankments on either side.

Or fly.

The officers reach her row. The older woman beside her is scanned first.

"Minimal cosmetic enhancements, registered three years ago," the officer reads from his device. "You're clear, ma'am."

"It was a gift from my daughter," she says. "So I can breathe underwater."

The scanner turns toward Paige. Her pulse pounds in her ears as the red beam passes over her body. The device emits a confused series of beeps, neither the clear tone of the enhanced nor the alert for unadjusteds.

CHAPTER ELEVEN

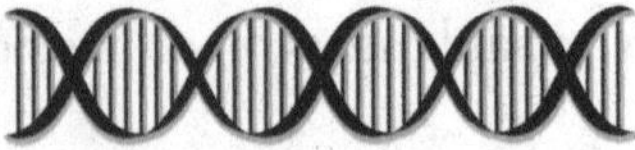

THE OFFICER FROWNS. "SCAN AGAIN," he instructs his colleague.

Same result.

"ID," the third officer demands, holding out his hand.

Paige passes over her card with fingers she forces not to tremble. The officer checks it against his tablet, eyes flicking between the screen and her face.

"No registered enhancements," he says, looking hard at her very obvious wings. "Stand up, please."

Paige rises slowly, aware of every eye on the bus now fixed on her. The officer gestures for her to step into the aisle.

"Where are you taking the unadjusteds?" Paige asks, buying seconds while her mind races.

"To a secure facility, as stated. Where did you get your nanite?"

"But where is this facility? What will happen to them there?"

The officer's patience evaporates. "That's classified information. Where did you get your nanite?"

The older woman across the aisle reaches up, touching Paige's arm gently. "Dear," she whispers, "don't make this harder."

Something in the woman's eyes , a mixture of fear and compassion, makes the decision for her. Paige glances toward the front of the bus. The door remains open, with only one officer standing near it, his attention now on the confrontation developing in the aisle.

"I'm sorry," Paige says to no one and everyone.

In one fluid motion, she dashes down the aisle. Gasps ripple through the bus as her wings stretch out. Before the stunned officers can react, she's moving, shoving past them, racing toward the front of the bus.

"Stop her!"

Paige barrels into the officer by the door, the momentum of her charge sending him sprawling across the steps. She leaps over him and into the cool night air, wings already extending to their full, impressive span. Air catches beneath them as she launches herself over the highway barrier.

The wind tears at Paige's face as she angles herself skyward, her wings beating frantically against the gravity trying to drag her back down to danger. The bus shrinks beneath her. Her heart hammers against her ribs so hard she swears the people below can hear it—if they weren't too busy shouting orders and aiming weapons at the sky.

Higher. She needs to get higher. The thought consumes her with the urgency of oxygen to drowning lungs. Each powerful downstroke of her wings sends tremors through the muscles of her back.

The emerald feathers catch the moonlight as she banks hard to the right, a flash of bright green against the dark sky. Too visible. Too exposed. But she can't stop now.

"Target the altered female! Priority capture!" The voice below sounds tinny and distant, but unmistakably threatening.

Paige pumps her wings harder, the air thinning as she climbs. Three hundred feet. Four hundred. Her lungs burn from the exertion and the altitude. She's only been flying for minutes but it feels like hours, her shoulders already screaming in protest. The bus checkpoint grows smaller, the uniformed figures becoming ant-like specks on the asphalt road.

The crack comes without warning. A sound like lightning striking too close. For one terrifying heartbeat, Paige thinks she's been hit. Her body instinctively tucks, wings folding partially as she rolls sideways, spiraling through the air in an evasive maneuver she didn't know she could perform.

The shriek that tears from her throat isn't human. It's primal, bird-like. Exactly what her DNA has become. Half-human, half-macaw. Not fully belonging to either world.

Another crack. This one sounds farther away. She's gaining distance. Her wings snap back open, catching an updraft that hurls her higher still, beyond the immediate range of whatever guns they're firing. But not beyond the range of her own fear, which chases her skyward like a predator.

They shot at her. Actually shot at her.

This isn't just discrimination anymore. This isn't just her parents ignoring her while they admire each other's new modifications in their floor-to-ceiling mirrors. This is something worse. Something that's been brewing beneath the surface of society for months now. The division between adjusteds and unadjusteds has finally erupted into violence.

Paige forces herself to look back, her neck craning uncomfortably as she maintains her altitude. What she sees freezes the blood in her veins. The unadjusteds from her bus being hurled into the waiting transport vehicle. One of the passengers protests. A NEA officer hits him on the head with the butt of his gun and the passenger goes down quicker than a brick in water.

Holy mother of God.

She can't bear to watch anymore. A shudder runs through her, and it has nothing to do with the cold air at this altitude. If she hadn't grown these wings, if she hadn't run away from her increasingly alien parents, she'd be down there too. Being loaded onto that transport vehicle with the others. Being taken to...where?

The thought stalks Paige's mind with more persistence than a hunter tracking wounded prey. Where are they taking them? What happens to unadjusteds now?

Her wings catch another thermal, lifting her higher with minimal effort. She needs to conserve her energy. The nearest resistance hideout is at least two days' flight away, and that's assuming perfect conditions and minimal rest. Matt and the others need to know what's happening. These roundups change everything. As well as the price on the Melodys' heads.

The hot updraft carries her in slow circles, giving her an aerial view of the region. From up here, the division of their world is laid bare.

As she flies, a single tear traces a path down her cheek, instantly whisked away by the rushing air. Not for herself, though her muscles already ache with the journey ahead, but for those below. For all the unadjusteds whose only crime was wanting to remain human.

"I'm coming," she whispers, though no one can hear her this high up. She drops her phone into a river far below. No one can trace her now. *Carson.* She expects she won't ever see him again. "I'm coming back for you."

CHAPTER TWELVE

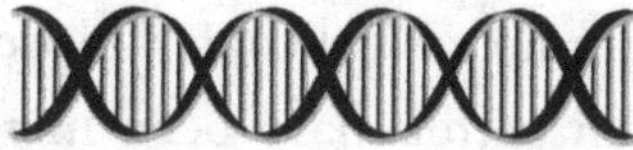

The forest looms ahead of Paige like a green sanctuary, its dense canopy promising cover from the helicopters that have buzzed overhead at regular intervals during her two-day flight. Her wings hang heavy, the muscles between her shoulder blades burning with an intensity that makes each downstroke feel like lifting concrete. Forty-eight hours of near-constant flying, grabbing only minutes of rest on remote rooftops and abandoned water towers, has pushed her modified body to its limits. Even nanite-enhanced physiology has breaking points, and she's dangerously close to finding hers.

She circles above the treeline, her emerald wings catching the late afternoon sunlight. The vast expanse of forest where the resistance hides their base stretches toward the coast. The sound of rotors in the distance makes the decision for her.

Paige tucks her wings and descends toward a small clearing at the forest's edge. Her landing is ungraceful, more controlled fall than proper touchdown, and her knees buckle as her feet hit the soft earth. For a moment, she simply kneels there, wings splayed out on either side, chest heaving as she gulps the oxygen her depleted muscles scream for.

"Just five minutes," she promises herself, voice cracking from dehydration. The water bottle she stole from a gas station yesterday is nearly empty, but she allows herself a small sip.

The distant thrum of helicopter blades grows louder. Government search patrols have been increasing since the roundups began. Paige forces herself to stand, wincing at the protest from her calves and thighs. The forest is her only option now, even if her wingspan makes movement beneath the canopy awkward at best, impossible at worst.

Unlike the carefully manicured forest parks near the adjusted zones, where trees are spaced to accommodate the increasingly exotic body modifications of the enhanced, this is wild country. Untamed. Unadjusted, like the humans being herded onto buses.

The forest swallows her as she steps beneath the first trees, the temperature dropping several degrees in the dappled shade. Her wings drag on the ground despite her best efforts to hold them folded tightly against her back. The nanite that gave her these wings didn't come with an instruction manual.

But function matters more than form right now, and twelve feet of wing makes moving through dense forest about as graceful as threading a needle while wearing boxing gloves.

Paige picks her way carefully through the underbrush, following what looks like a game trail. Each step forward is a victory against her fatigue. The sounds of the forest—birds calling, leaves rustling, the occasional snap of a twig beneath her feet—provide a stark contrast to the mechanical hum of the city traffic. Nothing manufactured here. Nothing enhanced or improved upon. Just nature, persistent and indifferent to humanity's genetic tinkering.

The thought brings unexpected comfort. This place doesn't care whether she has wings or not. Doesn't judge her for the choices that led her here. Doesn't see her as altered or natural, just another creature making its way through the undergrowth.

Her momentary peace shatters when her wing catches on a bramble. She gasps at the sudden pain of delicate feathers tearing. After extracting herself, she examines the damage. Three feathers bent, one pulled out completely. Not critical, but a reminder of her vulnerability.

"Next time I decide to grow wings, I'll pick something more practical for forest travel," she mutters to herself, then almost laughs at the absurdity. As if there would be a next time.

A branch snaps somewhere off to her left. Too loud to be a squirrel or rabbit. Paige freezes, her senses suddenly alert despite her fatigue. The forest has gone quiet. No birdsong. No rustling leaves. Just the sound of her own breathing, too loud in the sudden stillness.

Something's wrong.

She turns slowly, scanning the trees around her. Nothing moves. The forest holds its breath along with her.

Then she sees it. A shadow detaching itself from the deeper shadows between two ancient oaks. Hunched low to the ground. Four-legged. Much, much too big to be a wolf.

Is it a bear? But the animal has canine features. The hound's eyes lock onto hers, glowing amber orbs that seem to burn from within. The creature's shoulders stand as high as her waist, its massive head nearly as large as her torso. Most definitely modified. A modification designed for one purpose: hunting.

Hunting what, she doesn't have to guess. Hunting who.

A low growl rumbles from the beast's throat, unlike anything natural. It vibrates the air between them, making the fine hairs on Paige's arms stand on end.

Time slows as the hound gathers itself, powerful haunches tensing. Paige's options flash through her mind. She can't outrun it, can't fight it, can't hide from it.

But she can fly.

The creature lunges at the exact moment Paige's wings snap open. The action is instinctive, desperate, her wingspan hitting branches on both sides, feathers catching and tearing on twigs and leaves. The pain is immediate and sharp, but nothing compared to what those jaws would do if they closed around her leg.

The hound's slavering muzzle snaps closed inches from her ankle as she makes a frantic vertical leap, wings beating downward with all the strength her exhausted muscles can muster. The force is barely enough to lift her off the ground, not the clean takeoff she needs, but enough to buy precious seconds.

She claws at the lower branches above her, wings still beating frantically, trying to create enough lift in the confined space to escape. The hound circles below, growling that unnatural growl, watching with those burning eyes as she struggles. It leaps again, powerful hind legs propelling its massive body six feet into the air. Claws rake the side of her calf as she pulls herself higher, tearing through her jeans and leaving fire in their wake.

"No!" The word is both denial and desperate encouragement to herself as she climbs and flaps, climbs and flaps.

Twenty feet up now. The hound can only jump so high. But it doesn't leave. It circles the base of the tree, those amber eyes never leaving her. Waiting. Patient. Its handlers will come eventually. It's done its job—located the target.

Blood trickles down her leg. The cut isn't deep, but it stings. Above her, the canopy is dense. No chance of breaking through to open sky. To her right, though, a slight thinning of the branches. A possible path if she can reach it.

Paige edges along the branch she's perched on, keeping her eyes on the hound below. The creature matches her movement on the ground, staying directly beneath her. Intelligent. Too intelligent for comfort.

When she reaches the end of the branch, she gauges the distance to the next tree. Ten feet of open air. Not much for someone with wings in open space, but through these branches? She might as well be trying to fly through a maze blindfolded.

No choice. The hound's handlers could arrive any minute.

Paige launches herself toward the next tree, wings half-folded to fit through the gap, arms outstretched toward the nearest branch. For one heart-stopping moment, she's airborne, suspended between safety and a deadly fall back to the waiting predator.

Her hands close around rough bark. Her body slams against the trunk, driving the air from her lungs, but she holds on. Below, the hound snarls in frustration, pacing to keep her in sight as she pulls herself onto the new branch.

And then she runs. If you can call it running when you're twenty feet above the ground, leaping from branch to branch, half-flying and half-climbing, with a genetically modified predator tracking her every move below. Her wings catch and tear on branches, she scrapes her palms raw on rough bark, but she keeps going.

The hound maintains the pace easily, its muscular body flowing like liquid shadow beneath the trees. But it can't climb. Can't fly. As long as she stays above it, she has a chance.

The chase continues until the light begins to fade from the forest. Paige's strength is failing fast. She needs rest. Needs water. Needs to tend the claw wound on her leg before infection sets in.

When she can go no further, she chooses a massive oak with branches thick enough to support her weight comfortably. Climbing to where the trunk splits into three main branches, she finds a natural cradle. Not comfortable, but secure.

The hound settles at the base of the tree, those amber eyes glowing brighter as darkness falls. Watching. Waiting.

Paige's hands tremble as she tears strips from the bottom of her t-shirt to bind the wound on her leg. The bleeding has mostly stopped, but the area around the cuts is angry red and hot to the touch. She drinks the last of her water, knowing she'll need to find more tomorrow. Somehow.

Night deepens around her. The hound remains, a darker shadow against the darkness.

Occasionally its eyes close, but Paige doesn't fool herself that it's truly sleeping.

"You can wait all you want," she whispers down to it. "I'm not coming down."

She needs to sleep, but falling from this height would be fatal. With shaking hands, she unwraps the light jacket tied around her waist. It takes three attempts to tear it into strips, her fingers stiff with exhaustion. Working slowly, methodically, she creates a makeshift harness, securing herself to the branch.

It's awkward, uncomfortable, and the only thing keeping her from a deadly fall if she loses consciousness. Her wings make it harder. They don't fold completely flat against her back, meaning she has to position herself partly on her side, one wing carefully arranged over her like a blanket, the other wedged awkwardly beneath her.

The forest night is alive with sounds. Insects chirping, the occasional hoot of an owl, rustling as nocturnal creatures go about their business well above the reach of the hound. Paige listens, letting the natural rhythms soothe her frayed nerves.

Sleep comes in fragments, minutes of unconsciousness broken by startled waking, checking to make sure the hound is still below, adjusting her position to ease the cramps in her wings and back. It's the worst night's rest she's had since growing her wings, yet somehow still better than lying awake in her bedroom while her parents showed off their latest modifications to their equally altered friends downstairs.

Morning light filters through the leaves, painting dappled patterns across her skin. The hound is gone. Whether called away by its handlers or simply giving up the chase, Paige doesn't know. She doesn't trust its absence.

Her makeshift sleeping harness has left raw marks across her torso and under her arms, but it kept her alive. She unties herself slowly, wincing as circulation returns to compressed limbs.

"Keep moving," she tells herself, voice hoarse. "Just keep moving."

CHAPTER THIRTEEN

PAIGE SETTLES ON A THICK BRANCH, her back against rough bark, legs dangling in darkness. The forest feels safer than home these days, though *safe* is relative when hounds prowl below and President Bear's soldiers hunt for unadjusteds and troublesome altereds alike.

She secures herself to the branch with the scraps of her jacket. Three nights of sleeping in trees has taught her that even the most peaceful dreams can send you tumbling. Her fingers work methodically, tying the knot while her mind drifts homeward, and land on thoughts of Carson. Where is he? Has be been given a ticket number? Will he try to reach the hideout? Is he still gay? It's been almost two years since he was taken away.

Paige's heart aches with the need to see him. To hold him. To love him. Her best and only friend. The only one who ever saw her for who she truly was.

She swipes at her tears as she leans against the trunk. Sleep comes in fits and starts, her dreams slipping between memories of fishing with her dad before the cancer, before the nanites changed everything. In her dream, the river flows clear and cool, and her father's laugh isn't tinged with that manic edge it gained after his first enhancement.

Something sharp pricks her thigh, jolting Paige from sleep. She swats blindly in the darkness, her heart rate spiking as something skitters across her leg. Another bite, this time on her arm.

"No, no, no," she hisses, flailing. Her wing catches on a branch, and the sudden tension makes her jerk sideways. The tie around her waist slips from its mooring.

For one suspended moment, Paige hangs in space, her brain not yet processing the inevitable fall. Then gravity claims her.

Her wings flare instinctively, but the dense forest leaves no room for their full span. Branches scratch and tear at her as she plummets, each impact sending fresh jolts of pain through her body. She tries to angle herself, to somehow control the fall, but the forest is too tight, too close.

"Ahh!" The scream tears from her throat as she cartwheels through darkness, a wild pinwheel of limbs and wings in free fall. A spotlight suddenly catches her, highlighting her descent in stark white. Through her tumbling vision, Paige glimpses figures below, people with weapons raised toward her.

A thick branch strikes her midsection. "Oof!" The air rushes from her lungs as she performs an ungraceful circle around the branch before sliding off its far side.

Her fall slows but doesn't stop. When she finally hits the

ground, the impact drives what little breath she has left from her body. "Ouch."

Paige lies still, too dazed to move, too winded to speak. Her wings spread awkwardly around her like a crumpled green blanket. Through a haze of pain and confusion, she hears foot-steps approaching. The beam of a flashlight probes her prone form, and something—a stick, maybe—pokes at her wing.

Drawing a ragged breath into her protesting lungs, Paige forces herself to move. She peeks out from beneath the protective canopy of her wing to see several figures looming over her. One holds a gun, trained directly at her face. Another brandishes what looks like a machete.

"Don't shoot," she gasps, raising her hands in surrender. Her long hair, now tangled with twigs and leaves, cascades past her waist as she tries to sit up. "Don't shoot," she repeats, squinting against the harsh light.

The woman with the gun—older, with sharp cheekbones and a no-nonsense demeanor—steps closer, keeping both the gun and the light trained on Paige's face.

"Who are you?" the woman demands.

Paige shakes her shoulders, dislodging an assortment of forest debris from her wings. Leaves and twigs and pine needles shower down around her. "I'm Paige."

An older man with a mustache and intense blue eyes leans on what appears to be a makeshift crutch. "What are you doing here, Paige?" he asks, his accent hinting at German origins.

Paige glances up at the tree she fell from, her heart still hammering in her chest. "Was trying to sleep," she explains, rubbing her bruised ribs. "Something bit me. And I am not a fan of bugs, or rodents or whatever else might be in that tree." She shudders, remembering the creatures that had interrupted her dreams. "Or those horrible dogs and wolves running around the ground—"

"Hellhounds?" A young girl in a wheelchair asks, her expression more curious than frightened.

"Is that what they are?" Paige feels another shudder pass through her. "Well, I was in the middle of a dream, about fishing on the river way back home, and fell right out of that tree."

A young man with sandy brown hair and bright blue eyes steps forward, an amused smile playing on his lips. "You didn't think to use your wings?"

Heat rushes to Paige's cheeks. Of course it would seem ridiculous to someone who doesn't understand the mechanics of having actual wings. "I have a twelve-foot wingspan," she explains, gesturing to her folded plumage. "No way I could extend them up there. In here."

The blue-eyed boy nods. "Fair point."

"Where are you going?" the woman with the gun asks, her tone leaving no room for evasion.

Paige bristles at the interrogation. "I wasn't going anywhere. I was sleeping."

The woman edges closer, and Paige can now see the determined set of her jaw. "Are you saying you live in the forest?"

Paige notices the blue-eyed boy giving her a once-over. He's observant. Dangerous, maybe. More dangerous than the lady with the gun?

"It's a free country," Paige retorts.

The boy scoffs. "Is it?"

The question hangs in the air between them. They both know the answer. Not anymore. Not since President Bear's announcement about mandatory genetic enhancements.

"Maybe not anymore," Paige concedes, getting to her feet and narrowing her eyes. She feels vulnerable, outnumbered. "I don't have to tell you anything."

"I'm the one with the gun." The woman waves it in Paige's face, making her flinch.

The blue-eyed boy moves, edging around the older woman with careful, measured steps. There's something in his demeanor—a deliberateness, a thoughtfulness—that makes Paige think he might be more reasonable than his gun-wielding companion.

He offers what seems like a genuine smile, though Paige notices how his eyes dart periodically to the darkness surrounding them, alert to any noise.

"It's hard to trust anyone," he says, gesturing behind him where an older woman stands with her arm around a younger girl who, Paige realizes with a start, has white wings. He points to the wings. "We all feel a little like that."

Paige studies the group more carefully now. Most of them look...normal. Unaltered. "Wait, I thought you were all unadjusteds?" she asks, scanning the small gathering.

"Most of us are," the German man says, his grip on his makeshift weapon not relaxing one bit. "But that doesn't mean we're defenseless."

"No, of course not," Paige says quickly, taking in his stern expression. He reminds her of her soccer coach back home, before everything went sideways, before she stopped playing. Balanced. Centered. Serious. "Where are you all going?"

The spotlight finally moves away from her face, allowing Paige to see the blue-eyed boy more clearly. He's young, maybe around her own age, with an intelligent gaze that seems to be assessing her just as thoroughly as she's studying him.

"You first," he says.

Paige chews on her lip. She plucks a few more leaves from her wings, buying herself a moment to think. These people could be anyone. Bear's soldiers in disguise, altereds looking to score the next big enhancement by turning in unadjusteds. But something about them, about the boy especially, makes her want to trust them.

"Okay. I'm trusting you..." she says finally.

"And we you." The woman gestures again with the gun.

Paige zeroes in on the weapon, her teeth digging deeper into her lip. The cold metal of the barrel reflects the moonlight, reminding her how quickly things could go wrong.

The blue-eyed boy puts his hand on the barrel of the gun and gently pushes it downward. "She's unarmed."

"How can you tell?" the woman counters, not holstering the weapon. "She could have any number of weapons hidden within those wings."

Paige watches as the woman flicks the safety on. A small concession.

"I'm not hiding anything," Paige says, raising her hands once more. She shakes her wings, extends them as far as the forest clearing will allow while the woman combs the flashlight over every inch of her plumage. It's humiliating, being examined like a suspect, but Paige endures it. After what feels like an eternity, the woman seems satisfied.

With the immediate threat of being shot diminishing, Paige allows herself to hope these people might be part of the resistance.

"A friend of mine told me about a safe place to go," she says carefully. "Where unadjusteds are gathering—"

"You're not an unadjusted," the woman interrupts, her tone accusatory.

Paige feels the familiar shame wash over her. No, she's not. She chose her alteration. Chose it for all the wrong reasons.

"No," she admits. "But I wish I was. The wings..." She glances at her emerald feathers, remembering the desperation that drove her to the black market, to the older boy with the promising smile and the nanite pill that would make her parents finally see her. "Let's just say I went about it all wrong...I have regrets...and I don't think anyone should be forced into taking a nanite...my parents..."

Her voice cracks unexpectedly. She dips her chin, unable to continue for a moment as the familiar hurt wells up. "Sorry, that's another story for another time," she manages, hating how her voice trembles. "I have a habit of talking when I'm nervous. I heard about a cave where people are gathering. On the message boards? A resistance. A place where we can learn to fight back."

The blue-eyed boy's face transforms with a genuine smile. "That's where we're going too." He steps forward and offers his hand. "I'm Matt. This is Francesca," he gestures to the woman with the gun, "and Claus," the German man nods stiffly. "That's Megan in the wheelchair, Sofia with the wings, and my parents."

Matt? Matt *Lawson*? As in the name that's whispered on every forum as being one of the leaders of the resistance? She gives him another once over. She thought he'd be older. But strength comes in all sizes and ages. Maybe she can learn a little from him.

Paige shakes Matt's hand, feeling an unexpected warmth at the simple human contact. It's been weeks since anyone touched her with anything approaching kindness.

"Would you like to join us, or would you feel safer on your own?" Matt's mother asks, her voice gentle.

"We could use someone to scout ahead from the air," Claus adds, his practical tone suggesting he's already calculating how to use her abilities.

Paige feels something unfurl in her chest. Something light and warm that she hasn't felt since before her father got sick. Hope. Belonging. Purpose.

"I'd very much like to join you if you'll have me," she says, carefully folding her wings away.

"Are you on your own?" Megan asks, her young face curious.

Paige nods, unable to stop her eyes from glistening. "My parents...let's just say we see things differently."

"I'm sorry," Matt says, and something in his expression suggests he truly understands what it means to be torn from family. "Are you hurt?" He indicates the strips of cloth wrapped around her leg.

"Just a scratch," she lies, the heat of infection making her skin tight.

Before they go anywhere, Matt's mom makes her sit down. Matt gets a first aid kit out. They clean and re-bandage the wound, then give her a bottle of antibiotics. She cries. She can't remember the last time someone was so kind to her.

"Thank you." She wipes the tears from her cheeks.

Matt puts a hand on her shoulder. "We got your back."

As Paige gets to her feet and continues the journey with her new friends, she remembers the news she heard before taking flight into the forest.

"Did you guys hear about the compounds? And the price on the Melody's heads?" she asks.

Matt's reaction is immediate and visceral. His face drains of color, and he seems to struggle to remain upright. "Price? There's a price on their heads?"

The rest of the group share strained looks.

"A million each. Alive," Paige confirms, watching as the information ripples through the group. Whoever these Melody people are, they clearly matter to Matt.

As they amble through the forest, Paige feels a curious mix of emotions. Relief at finding companions. Caution at trusting too quickly. And beneath it all, a growing conviction that her wings, the very things she once regretted, might now serve a purpose greater than she ever imagined.

CHAPTER FOURTEEN

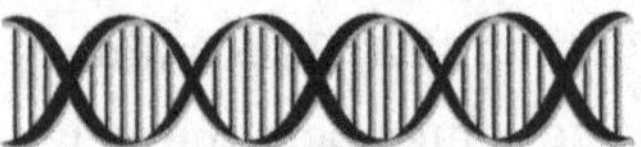

THE WIND WHIPS through Paige's hair as she soars above the forest canopy. She scans for movement, anything that might signal President Bear's forces closing in on their ragtag band of resisters. The unadjusteds and those who, like her, carry modifications they never wanted to become their whole identity.

It's been three days since she joined Matt and his group, three days of constant movement and watchful eyes, three days of antibiotics and healing wounds, but somehow it feels more like home than the hollow city she left behind.

She banks left, riding a thermal that carries her higher, giving her a wider view of the densely packed trees that stretch for miles in every direction. President Bear's troops could be anywhere, and the hellhounds—those genetically enhanced beasts with their unnatural speed and glowing eyes —have been spotted with increasing frequency.

A flash of movement pulls her attention back to earth. Paige narrows her eyes and hovers, spotting the telltale mechanical shimmer of a drone between the trees, its metallic body reflecting sunlight. President Bear's eyes and ears looking for unadjusteds to round up into compounds. She tucks her wings and dives, careful to stay within the shadow of a massive oak tree until she reaches the group below.

"Drone," she reports, landing with practiced grace beside Matt. She folds her wings away. "About half a mile west. Looks like a standard recon model."

Matt nods, his bright blue eyes analyzing the information with cool intelligence. "We'll adjust our route. Head south for a while." He turns to the others who have stopped to rest. Mr. and Mrs. Lawson check their packs while Francesca consults a battered paper ordinance map, no digital navigation that might be tracked.

Claus stands apart from the group, his posture alert and watchful. His gray mustache twitches as he scans the treeline.

"How long until we reach the cave?" Megan asks from her wheelchair, which her parents have been taking turns guiding over the uneven forest floor with the huge off-road wheels attached. At twelve, she's the youngest of their group, but her determination burns as bright as anyone's.

Paige crouches beside her. "By nightfall, if we're lucky. How are you holding up?"

"Better than Sofia," Megan grins, nodding toward the quiet ballet dancer who sits on a fallen log, massaging her feet through her worn slippers. Sofia, who usually dances with Megan's sister Lyla, had been caught in the roundup of unadjusteds. The ballet academy was raided, and while Sofia escaped, Lyla wasn't so fortunate. Paige watches Megan's smile falter for a moment before returning with fierce determination.

"I'm built for this," Megan says, patting the wheels of her chair. "Adjustable suspension. Can't say the same for pointe-trained feet on forest floors."

Paige smiles, admiring the girl's resilience. Megan could take a regeneration nanite to restore her legs, but she refuses. The wheelchair is part of her, she says. It doesn't define her, but it's not something to erase either.

"Ready to move out," Francesca announces, her no-nonsense tone brooking no argument. Her dark hair is pulled back in her signature messy bun, practical and severe. "Paige, can you scout ahead about a mile? We need to find a stream soon."

Paige nods and launches herself upward, powerful wing strokes lifting her above the canopy once more. The sensation thrills her, she's not too ashamed to admit that. She may not have a college degree, or parents who care, but she can fly.

She spots a glinting ribbon of water ten minutes later and circles back to guide the group. By the time they reach the stream, the afternoon has stretched toward evening. Mrs. Lawson helps Sofia with her blistered feet while Mr. Lawson and Matt refill water containers.

"Your wings," Claus says, appearing silently beside Paige as she dips her hands in the cool water. "They give you advantage in air. Disadvantage on ground."

She looks up. "I guess so. I never thought about it that way."

"We train now. Balance. Defense." His words are clipped

but not unkind. "Wings make you a target. You must learn to protect them."

Before she can protest, Claus leads her to a small clearing. The others watch with interest as the karate master demonstrates a basic stance as well as he can with a bullet wound in his leg.

"Feet shoulder width. Knees soft. Center low." He adjusts her posture with efficient movements. "Wings change your center. You must compensate."

For the next forty minutes, Paige learns to redistribute her weight, to account for the mass of her wings in defensive movements. What starts as awkward stumbling gradually transforms into something more fluid. By the time Claus calls a halt, sweat beads on her forehead, but a new confidence flows through her limbs.

"Good," is all he says, but she beams under the sparse praise.

Matt approaches with a canteen. "He doesn't waste words," he says, handing her the water. "But when Claus says 'good,' he means it."

Paige drinks gratefully. "He trained Silver too, right?"

Something shifts in Matt's expression at the mention of Silver's name, a softening around his eyes, a tension in his jaw. "Since we were kids. She's incredible. Black belt before she turned sixteen."

"You miss her," Paige says.

"Every day," Matt replies. "But she'll make it to the cave. She has to." He mutters the last, but Paige catches it.

She wants to ask more about Silver, this mysterious girl who seems to occupy such an important place in all their hearts, but Francesca calls them back to the group. It's time to move on.

As twilight settles over the forest, they make camp in a defensible position. Backs to a rock face, with clear sightlines in all directions. Paige takes the first watch, her wings giving her the advantage of height as she perches on a boulder. Below, the others prepare a small, smokeless fire.

From her vantage point, she watches the group interact. The Lawsons move with the coordinated ease of a family who know each other's habits by heart. Francesca and Claus confer in low voices, their serious expressions illuminated by firelight. Sofia helps Megan navigate from her chair to a comfortable spot by the fire. There's a rhythm to their movements, a sense of belonging that makes Paige's chest ache with longing.

"Room for one more?" Megan calls up to her, patting the space beside her log seat.

Paige hesitates, then folds her wings and jumps down. She settles beside the younger girl, who immediately offers her a portion of the simple meal Mrs. Lawson has prepared.

"Thanks," Paige says, accepting the food with genuine gratitude.

"So," Megan says, lowering her voice conspiratorially, "on a scale of one to dinosaur, how cool is it to fly?"

The question startles a laugh from Paige. "Definitely dinosaur level," she answers. "Though pterodactyls weren't actually dinosaurs."

"Nerd," Megan says affectionately.

Around the fire, conversation flows more freely than it has all day, tension easing as darkness provides a cover they don't have in daylight. Mr. Lawson talks about life before the nanites, their friendship with the Melodys and how everything developed. Francesca shares stories from her time on President Bear's Senate campaign, before he revealed his true agenda.

"He seemed so normal then," she says, her dark eyes reflecting the firelight. "Passionate about healthcare, education. No one suspected he'd use Margaret and Rufus' invention this way."

"Silver's parents," Megan explains to Paige. "They invented the nanite pill to help people. Now her mom's in prison for trying to stop the program, and Silver's on the run like us."

"Speaking of which," Mrs. Lawson says, "we should all get some rest. Long day tomorrow."

As the others settle into sleeping positions, Paige finds herself unable to relax. She keeps thinking about her own parents, wondering if they've noticed she's gone. Did they return from their vacation to find an empty house? Do they care? Or are they too busy admiring their own reflections to spare a thought for their daughter?

Sleep eventually claims her, but dawn comes too quickly. Paige wakes to Claus' hand on her shoulder, a silent signal it's time for her morning scouting flight. Her muscles protest. Yesterday's training session awakened new awareness in her body, but she pushes through the discomfort and takes to the air.

The sunrise paints the sky in gentle pinks and golds, a beautiful contradiction to the danger they're all in. Paige flies higher than usual, trying to get a sense of how far they still need to travel. According to Matt, the cave system is hidden in a valley ahead, a natural fortress that's been prepared as a haven for the resistance.

She spots something alarming on her return flight. Tracks in a muddy riverbank. Not human footprints, but the distinctive paw prints of hellhounds.

Paige dives back to the camp, where the others are packing up their meager supplies.

"Hellhound tracks," she reports breathlessly. "Fresh ones. Maybe six hours old, heading north."

"North is good," Matt says, shouldering his pack. "We're heading west. But they could pick up our scent if the wind changes."

"Then we move faster," Francesca decides, helping Sofia with her pack. "Paige, you and Claus take point. Matt, help with Megan's chair. Everyone else, single file, minimal talking."

The day passes in tense silence, broken only by necessary communication. Paige alternates between flying reconnaissance and walking with the group. During one of her ground stretches, she helps push Megan's chair through a particularly rough patch.

"You know what's funny?" Megan says quietly as they navigate around a fallen tree. "Everyone thinks I should want fixing. That a regeneration nanite would make me *normal* again." She makes air quotes with her fingers. "But this—" she pats her wheelchair "—this is my normal. Has been for two years."

Paige nods, understanding completely. "People look at my

wings and think I got them because I wanted to be special. They don't get that I just wanted to be seen."

"We see you," Megan says simply, reaching back to squeeze Paige's hand.

The simple statement hits Paige like a physical force, bringing unexpected tears to her eyes. She blinks them away quickly, focusing on the path ahead.

By late afternoon, the terrain grows increasingly difficult. The forest gives way to a steep downward gradient, and Megan's wheelchair becomes more challenging to maneuver. Without complaint, Mr. Lawson lifts his daughter onto his back while Matt folds and carries the chair.

"There," Francesca points as they crest a ridge. "That valley. The cave entrance is hidden behind that stand of pines."

Paige takes flight one last time, circling the area to ensure no one has followed them. The sky is beginning to darken with dusk, providing extra cover as the group makes their final approach to the cave entrance.

THE CAVE MOUTH yawns before them, a dark slash among darker trees that promises shelter from both the elements and President Bear's hunting parties. Paige steps inside first, her wings folded tight against her back to navigate the narrow entrance. The air shifts immediately. It's cooler, damper, and carries mineral scents that speak of hidden depths and ancient stone. As her eyes adjust to the dimness, the main chamber reveals itself: a cathedral-like space with a high ceiling that disappears into shadows, walls that glisten with trace minerals, and a surprisingly level floor smoothed by countless years of water flow. Lights flick on. Several LED lanterns hang from the walls on nails. Wires connecting them all are taped along the ground. It's not pretty, but it will do.

"Home sweet home," Matt says, helping Megan into her wheelchair once they've cleared the tight entrance passage. His voice echoes slightly, bouncing off the stone walls.

Francesca doesn't waste a moment on sentiment. "Check the emergency supplies," she directs, moving toward a stack of crates tucked against the far wall. "We should have basic provisions here from our last supply drop."

Paige watches as the group moves with practiced efficiency. They've been here many times over the last year, bringing supplies of food and weapons and clothing and first aid kits. To Paige's untrained eye, it looks like there are enough boxes to last them a lifetime. Until Matt tells her the cave can hold over four hundred people. Hopefully they will come.

"Want the tour?" Matt offers, hovering beside Paige.

"Lead the way," Paige says, grateful for the guidance.

Matt leads her over smooth wooden planks he laid on a previous visit to accommodate Megan's wheelchair. He points out features of the main chamber. "This is where we gather, eat, plan our resistance efforts. Very dramatic for speeches," he adds with a grin, his voice rising to demonstrate the echo effect.

They move toward a narrow passage on the right side of the chamber. "Sleeping quarters through here," he explains. "Natural alcoves, some big enough for families, others just for one or two people. I rigged up some privacy curtains last time I was here."

Paige peeks into the passage, seeing fabric hanging at intervals, creating separate spaces within the continuous rock corridor. Simple sleeping pads and bags lie in some alcoves, while others remain empty.

"We're the first to arrive," he says. "Others will come. Those who couldn't make the journey with us or who had to take different routes to avoid detection."

"Like Silver?" Paige asks.

Something crosses Matt's face. Pain? "Yeah. Silver and her dad. We need him. When they get here, things will really start happening."

They continue the tour, with Matt leading Paige down another passage that slopes gently downward. The sound of water grows louder, and the air becomes more humid.

"And this," he announces as they emerge into a wide, low-ceilinged chamber, "is our luxury spa facilities."

An underground lake spreads before them, its still surface reflecting the soft glow of lanterns placed around the edges. The water is crystal clear, revealing a sandy bottom that slopes gradually deeper.

"It's fed by an underground spring," Matt says. "Clean enough to drink and warm enough to bathe in without freezing to death. One of nature's perfect gifts to the resistance."

Paige extends her wings, feeling how the humidity eases the tension in her feathers. "It's beautiful," she says softly.

"Yeah," he agrees. "Almost makes you forget there's a megalomaniac president trying to force everyone to take DNA-altering pills."

They return to the main chamber where the others have begun organizing supplies. Mr. and Mrs. Lawson unpack food provisions while Claus inspects the perimeter of the cave, checking for security vulnerabilities. Francesca and Matt huddle over maps and communication equipment, speaking in low, urgent tones.

"Not as much as I'd hoped," Mrs. Lawson announces, gesturing to the food supplies. "We need to organize a run soon."

Paige steps forward. "I can help. My wings give me a good vantage point for scouting safe routes."

Francesca looks up from her maps, assessing Paige with sharp eyes. "We'll wait for Kyle. He knows the terrain and nearby towns. Should be here tomorrow if he wasn't intercepted."

The first night in the cave passes slowly. Paige chooses a small alcove for herself, hanging a curtain for privacy though she leaves it open for now. She unfolds her sleeping bag on the surprisingly comfortable stone shelf that will serve as her bed. From her pack, she pulls the only personal item she brought from home, the photograph of her and her parents before they all took nanites.

Sleep comes fitfully, her dreams filled with flying and falling, with her parents' transformed faces turning away from her no matter how loudly she calls to them. With Carson.

Morning brings a flurry of activity as everyone settles into roles. Paige helps Mrs. Lawson inventory their supplies while Megan and Sofia organize the sleeping quarters, making space for expected arrivals. By mid-afternoon, Paige takes a flight outside to stretch her wings and scan the surroundings.

She's circling back toward the cave entrance when movement below catches her eye, a figure moving with unnatural speed through the trees. Her first instinct is to sound an alarm, but something about the movement pattern seems deliberate, controlled. Not a hellhound or soldier, but someone who knows where they're going.

Paige dives lower, wings creating enough noise to alert

the figure. A young man looks up, his hazel eyes widening at the sight of her green wings before a grin splits his face.

"Dude, talk about making an entrance," he calls up. "You must be the wing girl Matt told me about over the radio."

Paige lands, folding her wings carefully. "And you must be Kyle."

"The one and only," he confirms, adjusting the heavy backpack he carries. He's shorter than Matt but has a toned physique that speaks of hours in a gym. "Nice to meet a fellow altered who didn't drink the President's Kool-Aid."

"Right back at you," she says with a smile. "The cave's this way," she says, gesturing toward the hidden entrance.

"I know," Kyle replies with easy confidence. "Been making this trek since we established the hideout last year. But I wouldn't say no to an aerial escort."

Paige takes to the air again, circling above Kyle as he makes quick work of the remaining distance to the cave. His enhanced speed, a gift from the nanite he took for track and karate competitions, gives him a fluid, effortless gait even on the uneven terrain.

Kyle's arrival brings new energy to the cave. He distributes items from his backpack—medicine, batteries, ammunition for Francesca's gun, and, to everyone's delight, fresh fruit and chocolate.

"Raided my parents' stockpile," he explains as Megan bites into an apple with obvious pleasure. "They won't report it missing. They think I'm at a training camp for enhanced athletes."

Later that evening, Kyle approaches Paige as she sits near

the entrance, enjoying the fresh air that circulates from outside.

"Francesca says we need to make a supply run tomorrow," he says, dropping down beside her. "You up for it? Having someone who can scout from above would make things a lot easier."

"Sure," Paige agrees, surprised by how quickly she's being integrated into their operations. "What exactly are we looking for?"

"Food, mostly. Dry goods. Medical supplies if we can find them. There's a small town about five miles west that's been sympathetic to unadjusteds. They leave supplies in drop locations for us."

Kyle explains the system they've developed, a network of supporters who leave packages in predetermined locations. Sometimes it's farmers with extra produce, other times it's pharmacy employees who can spare bandages and antibiotics.

"It's not much," Kyle admits, "but it's going to help us survive."

Dawn finds Paige and Kyle setting out for their supply run. The early morning air is crisp against Paige's face as she flies high above, scanning for patrols or surveillance drones. Below, Kyle moves through the forest with his enhanced speed, staying under the canopy where possible.

They reach the first drop point—a hollow tree trunk marked with a small, almost invisible symbol—without incident. Kyle retrieves a waterproof bag containing canned goods and dried fruit.

"Two more stops," he tells Paige when she lands beside

him. "Then we hit the stream to check the fish traps Matt set up last month."

The routine of their days establishes itself quickly. Paige alternates between scouting flights, supply runs with Kyle, and training sessions with Claus. In the main chamber of the cave, the group gathers for meals and strategy meetings, planning how to resist President Bear's increasingly aggressive policies against unadjusteds.

A week passes. More resistance members arrive in ones and twos. A doctor who refused to administer forced nanites to children, a teacher who was fired for teaching about bodily autonomy, families who fled rather than submit to mandatory enhancements. A bulk, an ex-pro ball player. And a girl with shimmering butterfly wings that change color according to her emotions. The cave's population grows to nearly a hundred people.

Paige is returning from a scouting flight when Matt rushes past her toward the cave entrance, his usually calm demeanor replaced by barely contained excitement.

"She's here," is all he says as he passes.

Paige follows inside to see a slim figure standing in the middle of the main chamber, a girl with dark hair and striking silver eyes that catch the light even at a distance.

Silver Melody has arrived. Not with her father, but with a bulk ball player. *Ex*-ball player.

The main chamber buzzes with energy. Everyone seems to gravitate toward her. Not because she demands attention, but because she carries a quiet intensity that draws people in. Paige watches from the periphery as Silver hugs the Lawsons, clasps hands with Francesca, and exchanges a solemn nod with Claus.

When Silver turns to Matt, something electric passes between them, a moment of connection so palpable Paige almost feels like an intruder for witnessing it. They don't embrace, but the way Silver's hand rests briefly on Matt's arm speaks volumes.

"I'm so glad you're here," Matt says, his voice thick with emotion.

"Me too," Silver replies, her silver eyes scanning the cave. "Nice setup."

Kyle appears at Paige's side, his hazel eyes bright with amusement. "Watching the Matt and Silver show?" he whispers. "Been running for years. Neither of them will admit it, but everyone knows."

"Knows what?" Paige asks, though she already suspects the answer.

"That they're crazy about each other," Kyle confirms. "Have been since before the nanite crisis. Matt's been in love with her forever. Silver...well, she's harder to read, but it's there."

Dinner that night feels like a celebration despite the circumstances that have brought them together. And that fact that Silver's father has been abducted.

Mrs. Lawson manages to create a feast from their limited supplies, and even Francesca's stern expression softens as she shares a glass of precious wine with Claus and the other adults.

Paige finds herself seated beside Silver, finally getting a

chance to properly meet the girl everyone speaks of with such reverence.

"Your wings are beautiful," Silver says, as she devours a roll and a bowl of soup.

"Thank you," Paige replies, and means it. There's something about this girl, a kindness, a warmth, a compassion, and Paige knows she's going to be her friend. "With more of the unadjusteds in compounds, the supply drops have slowed. I've talked Francesca into a supply run tomorrow. We're going to hit a warehouse on the edge of town. I hear you can handle yourself with a knife?"

She nods.

Matt pokes her ribs. "When did that happen? Being a black belt wasn't enough for you?"

She flicks his knee and Paige watches the easy camaraderie between them, wishing she had that too, wishing she had Carson.

"Would you like to come with us?" Paige asks.

"Absolutely."

As they eat, they sit in comfortable silence, two girls whose lives have been shaped by forces beyond their control, both finding ways to reclaim their agency.

"I'm glad you're here, Paige," Silver says. "We need people who understand both sides. Who've taken enhancements but still believe in choice."

The validation washes over Paige like warm sunlight. In her parents' house, filled with artificial enhancements and hollow conversations, she had been invisible. Here, in a cave filled with strangers fighting for their right to remain unaltered, her altered self has found belonging.

"I'm glad I'm here too," she says, and means it more than anything she's said in years.

)O(O(O(

If you want to know what happens to Paige once she meets up with Silver and team, don't forget to check out *The Unadjusteds*:

https://geni.us/Theunadjusteds

Read on for the first chapter in the next origin story, *Hal Small...*

FACEBOOK READERS GROUP

If you want to experience more of my books, do join my Facebook readers group where you can chat to other readers and discuss my books, as well as anything else you are reading. I am very active in this group, and you can expect book jokes, puzzles, riddles, quizzes, giveaways, the opportunity to name characters, as well as secret information about what I'm working on, cover reveals and so much more!

Just click here: https://www.facebook.com/groups/840324970233576

Read on for the first chapter in the next origin story, *Hal Small.*

If you'd like to read the next book in the series for **FREE**, please sign up to my newsletter at

https://www.marisanoelle.com/subscribe/

Don't forget there are 10 more companion novellas in the series:

Silver Melody

Matt Lawson

Joe Rucker

Erica Swiftfield

Hal Small

Kyle Lewis

Jacob Shea

Sawyer Watson

Addison Shields

President Bear

Read on for the first chapter in the next origin story, *Hal Small*...

HAL SMALL
An Unadjusteds Story
MARISA NOELLE

Hal Small lost everything the day the enhancements became mandatory—his wife, his child, his faith in the system.

He was once a football star—enhanced, powerful, unstoppable. But when a government mandate forces all unadjusted citizens to submit to nanite modification, Hal's world shatters. His wife is murdered. His son is taken. And his strength means nothing against the machine of control.

Now a fugitive hiding in the Great Woods, Hal joins a growing resistance of outcasts, rebels, and altered allies with nothing left to lose. Together, they train for the fight of their lives—against a regime determined to erase the unenhanced, and a future where choice is no longer an option.

But can one broken man turn his grief into a weapon powerful enough to take down an immortal army?

What does it take to stay human in a world that no longer values humanity?

HAL SMALL
CHAPTER ONE

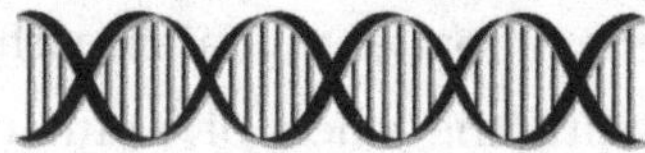

Hal's future is waiting.

It's all right in front of him, just waiting for him to grab it. If he plays well, that four-year contract with regeneration nanites will be his. Maybe a shoe or a drink commercial too. He'd love to snag a deal with BioBurst, because not only does it boost performance, it actually tastes good too.

Adrenaline courses through his veins as Hal scans the field. It's a familiar companion. One he relishes. The roar of the crowd swells around the stadium, sixty thousand voices melding into a single entity hungry for the spectacle of enhanced bodies colliding at superhuman speeds. Hal adjusts his helmet, his body humming with energy, ready to run and dive and smash his opponents.

He still marvels at the strength in his body, the gifts the nanite gave him. It's been nearly ten years since he took the bulk nanite, but every night he thanks his lucky stars.

"Ready to crush it, Small?" Coach Decker slaps Hal's

shoulder pad, his weathered face creasing into what passes for a smile.

"You bet." And he is. Because he's playing on his home ground. The field he's come to love over the last seven years is his second home. His team? The Central City Reapers. Two Super Bowl wins. It doesn't get much better than that.

The tunnel vibrates with the stomping of feet above, the crowd growing impatient. Hal breathes in the recycled air, tinged with the smell of industrial cleaner and sweat. Beside him, the other players paw at the ground like racehorses straining to be released. Only three players on their team remain unadjusted—Miller, Jackson, and Ramirez—scattered like dandelions among a field of steel. Their bodies are noticeably leaner, their eyes a touch more anxious. There's a fragility to them that the nanite-enhanced players don't possess, a reminder of human limitations in a sport that increasingly demands more than humanity was designed to give.

"Let's make them work for their paychecks today," Dominguez murmurs, the team's star receiver, nodding toward the Baltimore Barons waiting at the other end of the field. His skin shimmers with a faint copper glow—an unnecessary aesthetic addition to his class-8 reflex enhancement, but one that makes him instantly recognizable to fans and merchandise buyers. And boy, does he rake in the money with his royalties.

The signal comes, and they burst from the tunnel into blinding light. The crowd explodes, the sound physical enough to push against Hal's chest. He raises a hand, acknowledging their cheers, using their energy to fuel his determination.

The field stretches before them, impossibly green and perfect. Hal's cleats bite into the turf as they warm up, his muscles loosening with each practiced movement. Across the field, the Barons' defensive line looks formidable—all bulk-enhanced, their shoulders broad, necks thick as tree trunks. Hal spots only one unadjusted player on their side, a kicker with a slender frame that looks almost childlike among the enhanced giants.

"National anthem," Coach barks, and they line up along the sideline, hands over hearts. Hal catches Jackson wincing as he raises his arm, a lingering injury from last week that would have healed instantly with regeneration nanites, but Jackson's contract doesn't cover the expensive treatment. The divide in the league is only growing.

The coin toss goes their way. Offense first.

In the huddle, quarterback Martinez's eyes gleam with an intimidating golden sheen. "Spider-two Y banana, on two. Hal, you're the primary look if they show blitz."

Hal nods, already visualizing the route, the defender's likely movements, the small window of opportunity that will open for precisely 0.8 seconds. His bulk enhancement isn't just about strength—it's about precision, about applying exactly the right amount of force at the right moment.

"Break!"

They explode from the huddle into formation. Across the line of scrimmage, the Baron's middle linebacker—a moun-tain of a man with dermal reinforcement nanites that make his skin look like polished granite—points directly at Hal.

"Eighty-eight! Watch eighty-eight!"

Hal smiles behind his face mask. They always watch him, and he still finds ways to make them pay.

"Hut! Hut!"

The ball snaps and time slows. This is where the bulk nanites truly shine, enhancing not just his strength but his perception. While an unadjusted player might see chaos, Hal sees patterns, trajectories, opportunities—his brain working overtime. The defensive end crashes down, leaving a gap. Hal erupts through it, muscles generating force that would tear normal human tendons from bone.

The linebacker meets him five yards downfield, a collision that sends a shock wave through the stadium. The seconds stretch on as they're locked together. The taste of grass and dirt fills Hal's mouth. It's not entirely unpleasant. The linebacker grunts. Then Hal feels the subtle shift of weight, the microsecond of imbalance. He drives his legs, pushes with calculated force, and suddenly he's free, running to freedom and glory.

Fifty yards later, the crowd is on its feet, and Hal is in the end zone, ball raised triumphantly.

First touchdown of the game. He doesn't dance or pose, just hands the ball to the official and jogs back to the sideline, accepting high-fives as he goes.

"That's what I'm talking about!" Martinez slaps his helmet. "They can't stop the freight train!"

Coach Decker just nods, as if the play was expected. "Good read, Small. Good execution."

The game flows on. Nearing halftime, the Reapers lead 21-14, with Hal responsible for two touchdowns. Hal winces as an enhanced wall of muscle tears into Jackson, sending him sprawling across the turf. But as his unadjusted teammate struggles to his feet, the fire in his eyes shows his determination.

But it's only five minutes later when Jackson finds himself in the crosshairs of one of the Barons' enhanced linebackers. The linebacker charges at Jackson with an intensity that sends shivers through the crowd.

The moment stretches into eternity as spectators hold their breaths in anticipation. Hal holds his breath too. Then, with an impact that echoes across the stadium, they collide.

Jackson crumples as if he were made of paper rather than flesh and bone. His knee twists unnaturally under him, buckling under the force of the tackle. A sickening snap cuts through the air. A sound no one ever wants to hear on a football field.

The crowd gasps collectively as realization dawns; that was not just any noise but the gruesome rip of tendons tearing. The stadium falls silent, save for Jackson's agonized groan echoing hauntingly across the field.

Hal jogs over to him. Jackson blinks in recognition, grips Hal's outstretched hand, squeezes all his pain into it. Hal can take it. Hell, he can barely feel it.

"Just breathe," Hal tells him. "Breathe through the pain."

Jackson rasps for breath. A couple minutes later medics come out with a stretcher. Hal lifts his teammate onto the stretcher and watches as he's carted away. He catches eyes with Miller, sees the fear in his eyes, knowing it could have been him. The football field is no longer a place for unadjusteds. But most of them can't afford the bulk nanite or are still saving up for it. He likes Jackson. And Miller and Ramierz. He doesn't want them to get hurt, and he knows they'd all refuse to step down. But they're going to get hurt if they stay.

There's only one more play until the halftime whistle sounds. Neither team scores.

"Should've gotten bulked up." Hal overhears one of the rookie enhanced players mutter about Jackson as Hal heads to the locker room. "What's he thinking, playing natural against bulks?"

Hal frowns but says nothing. As he grabs a cup of water, he spots Jackson in the rehab room. A team of doctors with grim expressions are working on him as his mouth twists with pain. Without regeneration nanites, he's likely done for the game, maybe longer.

"You're killing them out there, Small." Coach finds him by the water fountain, droplets carelessly dribbling down his chin. "They've got no answer for your power game."

Hal nods, but his eyes drift to Jackson, now wearing a brace on his knee. "What's the word on Jackson?"

Coach's face tightens. "MCL sprain. He's done today."

"His contract cover regen nanites?"

"That's between him and management." Coach turns away, but the answer is clear enough. Lower-tier players, especially unadjusted ones, rarely get the premium medical benefits. Hal sends up a quick prayer that he had the foresight to sign with a fantastic agent who made sure his contract took care of him. And he's going to make damn sure his new contract comes with all the bells and whistles.

The second half begins with renewed intensity. The Barons adjust their defense, double-teaming Hal on every play. It creates opportunities for others, but the physical toll mounts. Ramirez takes a brutal hit over the middle, his unadjusted body crumpling under the impact of a member of the opposition whose reflexes and strength have been enhanced to the legal limit. Or maybe beyond. More and more documents are being forged, signed off by doctors with a wad of cash sent under the table.

The crowd gasps, then falls silent as medical staff rush onto the field. Hal watches, the familiar unease coiling in his stomach. Ramirez eventually sits up, woozy but conscious, and is helped off the field.

Two unadjusted players down, one remaining. The disparity has never felt more stark.

With six minutes left in the fourth quarter and the score tied at 28, Miller, the last unadjusted Reaper still playing, fumbles after a jarring hit. The Barons recover and score, taking the lead. Miller is subbed out. He sits alone on the bench, head in his hands, while the enhanced players avoid eye contact.

"Not his fault," Hal says to Martinez, as they prepare for the final drive. "Any of us would've dropped it after a hit like that."

Martinez raises an eyebrow. "Maybe. But that's kind of the point, isn't it? We don't take hits like that."

Two-minute warning. Down by seven. Eighty yards to go.

This is where Hal earns his contract. On first down, he breaks three tackles for a twelve-yard gain. Second play, he pancakes a blitzing linebacker, giving Martinez time to find Dominguez for thirty yards. The stadium thrums with energy as they cross midfield.

"They're tired," Hal says in the huddle, tasting victory. "Front side's overplaying. Counter will be there."

Martinez nods. "Counter 38 Blast on one. Ready? Break!"

The play unfolds like a dream. The defensive line shifts exactly as Hal predicted, overcommitting to his initial movement. He takes the handoff, plants his foot, and cuts back against the grain. One defender has stayed home—their free safety, an enhanced player known for his closing speed.

Their gazes collide. They are alone in space, a one-on-one confrontation that will decide the game. The safety launches himself, a perfectly timed missile. But energy sings in Hal's veins, and he makes a cut that should be impossible for a man his size. The safety grazes him, fingers sliding off his jersey, and then there's nothing but open field.

Sixty thousand fans rise as one as Hal crosses the goal line. Tie game, thirty seconds left. The extra point gives them the lead, and the defense holds for a dramatic victory. Four more years. All of Hal's dreams are coming true. He looks up at the stands, sees his wife holding their sleeping son, and smiles. He wishes he could pause this moment and stay in it forever.

In the locker room, champagne flows. Hal accepts congratulations and banter with his teammates, but his eyes keep drifting to the training room where team doctors work on Jackson and Ramirez.

"MVP! MVP!" The chant starts with Dominguez and spreads through the locker room. Coach Decker appears with the game ball.

"No surprise here. Player of the game...Hal Small!"

The ball lands in his hands to thunderous applause. Hal

raises it briefly, acknowledging the honor. As the cameras flash and reporters press forward, he can't help thinking about the players in the training room, wondering if their contracts might suddenly include regeneration nanites if they'd made the game-winning play instead.

"How does it feel, Hal?" asks a reporter, thrusting a microphone toward him.

Hal chooses his words carefully. "Just doing my job. Team victory today."

"Are you going to let anyone else get a few seconds in the limelight?" a pretty, blonde reporter asks.

"Always happy to share," Hal replies.

"And he's far too modest for his own good," Coach cuts in. "You won that game, and I think you'll find the powers that be may have to add another zero to that contract."

Hal can't help but grin. That would set him and Mara up for life. And they could start a college fund for Brandon.

Coach drags him and a couple of other players into the press room. Hal has been in here countless times before, but he never gets used to the brightness of the lights or the sound of the cameras clicking.

He sits at the center of the long table, and smiles politely at the forest of microphones.

"Hal, that's your third straight game with over a hundred fifty yards," calls out a reporter from the front row, her eyes glowing with inhuman light. "Does it feel like you're reaching a new level this season?"

"Offensive line is creating great opportunities. Martinez is making the right reads. It's a team effort," Hal replies.

"But you're the one making the impossible plays," another

reporter chimes in. "That cut on the final touchdown... physics says a man your size shouldn't be able to change direction that quickly."

Hal shifts slightly. "That's what the nanites are for, I guess."

"Speaking of which," an older reporter leans forward, "three unadjusted players were injured today. Do you think there's still a place for naturals in the modern game?"

The question hangs in the air. Hal feels a flicker of annoyance at the term "naturals," the subtle implication that enhanced players are somehow unnatural.

"Jackson, Ramirez, and Miller are elite athletes who've earned their spots on this team. The game's evolving, sure, but football has always been about more than physical attributes. It's about heart, intelligence, work ethic."

"But realistically," the reporter presses, "given the speed and strength of enhanced players, isn't it irresponsible to field unadjusted players? For their own safety?"

"I think everyone deserves the right to choose," Hal says, his voice firmer now. "Some players have religious objections to nanites. Some have medical contradictions. Some just want to play the game as they are. That's their decision."

Coach Decker leans in. "Two more questions, folks. We've got a bus to catch."

After fielding softballs about next week's matchup, Hal escapes the press room, nodding appreciatively at the staff who hold doors for him. The stadium corridors are quieter now, most fans departed, but team personnel and security still bustle about. Outside the locker room, he pauses when he hears raised voices.

"—league minimum for what? To watch him get carted off every other game?" It's Thornton, one of the defensive tackles, his voice carrying through the half-open door. "Management needs to stop wasting roster spots on unadjusteds."

Hal's jaw tightens at the edge in Thornton's tone.

"Miller's got a wife and kid," someone else replies. "Not everyone won the nanite lottery like you did at USC."

"Not my problem," Thornton says. "Football's an enhanced sport now. Unadjusteds should stick to, I don't know, badminton or whatever."

Hal pushes the door open. The conversation stops abruptly as he enters. Thornton has the decency to look embarrassed, but doesn't back down.

"Just saying what everyone's thinking, Small."

"Not what I'm thinking," Hal replies, keeping his voice level despite the anger simmering beneath. "Those unadjusteds you're talking about? They're our teammates. They bleed for this team same as you."

"Yeah, difference is they bleed a lot more," another player chimes in, earning scattered laughter.

Hal opens his locker, shoulders tight. "Easy to talk big when you've got class-nine durability nanites, isn't it? Some guys make a choice not to enhance. Others can't afford it. Either way, they deserve respect."

"It's not about respect," Thornton argues. "It's about reality. The game's faster, harder than it was twenty years ago. Unadjusteds can't keep up without getting wrecked. That's just facts."

"I wouldn't be here without my bulk enhancement," Hal

admits, fishing his street clothes from his locker. "But I got lucky. Junior year of high school, community raffle for one class-ten nanite. One in ten thousand odds, and I hit it. Without that? Who knows."

The locker room quiets, players listening now. Hal rarely talks about how he got his enhancement.

"Before that, I was just another kid from the east side with decent hands and average speed," he continues, pulling on his shirt. "My parents couldn't have afforded a basic class-three, let alone a bulk. So when I see guys like Miller playing unadjusted? That's not weakness. That's courage."

Thornton looks away, not quite convinced but unwilling to argue further. "Whatever, man. Just hate seeing guys carted off when a simple pill could prevent it."

The conversation shifts to safer topics as Hal finishes changing. He checks his phone. There's a message from Mara asking if he'll be late. He texts back that he has to make an appearance at the VIP reception but will be home soon after. As he pockets his phone, he notices Jackson hobbling in, knee heavily braced.

"Hey," Hal says, moving to help him to his locker. "How bad?"

"Grade two MCL sprain," Jackson replies, grimacing as he sits. "Eight weeks, minimum."

"Your contract cover regen nanites?"

Jackson laughs without humor. "What do you think? I'm a fifth-round pick on a rookie deal. I'm lucky they're paying for the MRI."

Hal nods, understanding all too well. "Season's not over. You'll be back."

"Maybe," Jackson says, but they both know the truth, eight weeks on the sideline means his roster spot might not be waiting for him when he returns.

They shake hands and Hal pulls him in for a one-armed hug before he leaves for the swanky reception.

The VIP lounge glitters with wealth, the air perfumed with expensive colognes and enhanced pheromones. Sponsors and season ticket holders mingle with players, the social hierarchy as visible as the quality of their clothing. Hal navigates the space, accepting congratulations, signing the occasional autograph, posing for photos with wide-smiling executives.

"There he is!" A portly man with artificially whitened teeth waves Hal over. "The man of the hour!"

Hal recognizes him as Ellison, a major team sponsor whose security company provides facial recognition systems to several stadiums. Beside him stands another executive, thin and severe looking.

"Incredible performance today, Small," Ellison says, pumping Hal's hand. "Simply incredible."

"Thank you, sir. I appreciate that. It's always nice to hear good things."

"Nice?" Ellison laughs. "Jersey sales up thirty percent this quarter! That's better than *nice*."

The thin executive eyes Hal with professional assessment. "The bulk enhancement is Nanocorp's model $B1.0$, correct? How long have you had it?"

"Since high school," Hal replies. "About twelve years now."

"Remarkable longevity," the man nods approvingly. "Most

first-generation bulks show degradation after a decade. You must have exceptional genetic compatibility."

Hal shrugs, heat pooling on the back of his neck. "Guess I'm lucky."

"More than lucky," Ellison says. "Smart! Not like these young idiots still trying to play unadjusted. Did you see that fumble today? Shameful."

Something cold settles in Hal's stomach. "Miller took a hit that would've broken an enhanced player's ribs. The fact he held onto the ball as long as he did was impressive."

Ellison waves dismissively. "If he can't afford enhancement, he shouldn't be in the league. It's irresponsible."

"Not everyone wants enhancement," Hal says quietly.

They both look at him blankly, reassessing. The cool of the air conditioning funnels down Hal's shirt, but it does nothing to thaw the heat on his cheeks.

"Then they need to get out of the game," Ellison says.

The thin man nods. "The league is evolving. Unadjusted players are becoming a liability. Insurance rates, injury time-outs disrupting game flow, negative fan perception when stars are sidelined."

"When I was coming up, I couldn't have afforded enhancement," Hal says. "If I hadn't won that raffle, I'd have been just another kid with potential who never got the chance. Is that the future we want? Where only the wealthy get enhancements and opportunities?"

An uncomfortable silence falls. Ellison's smile becomes fixed.

"Well," he says finally, "I should mingle. Wonderful game today, Small. Truly wonderful."

Hal curses as they walk away. He's media trained. He knows how to nod along like one of the dashboard toys. But why didn't he? Because he's sick of the injustice, of the growing divide, of the way people might treat his unadjusted wife. She's never complained, never mentioned prejudice, but now Hal wonders.

A hand claps his shoulder, and he turns to find Pearson, the team's general manager, standing behind him.

"Easy on the social justice, Small," Pearson says, his tone light but his eyes serious. "Ellison's company is up for contract renewal next season."

"Sorry," Hal says, not feeling particularly sorry. "Just tired of the attitude."

Pearson guides him to a quieter corner. "Look, I get it. But you need to understand the direction the league is heading. Fans want spectacle. Sponsors want reliability. Both mean more enhancements, not fewer."

"And players who choose to remain unadjusted, or can't afford enhancement?"

"The market decides," Pearson says with the finality of someone stating an immutable law. "Just like it always has."

Later, as Hal waits for his car at the VIP exit, he watches a group of fans gathered behind the security barrier. Children wave jerseys and footballs, hoping for autographs. One boy, no more than ten, wears Hal's number 88. Beside him, a slightly older girl holds a sign: "MILLER #17 - UNADJUSTED HERO."

Hal walks over, signs their items, poses for photos. The girl with the Miller sign beams at him.

"My dad says Miller's the bravest player because he

doesn't use nanites," she tells Hal. "He says that's real football."

Hal smiles, but inside, his unease grows. He wonders how long *real football* will exist for players like Miller, Jackson, and Ramirez. How long before the economics that Pearson speaks of with such certainty reshape the game completely? And what responsibility does he, with his lucky bulk enhancement, have to those left behind?

To carry on reading, click here:
https://geni.us/HalSmall